SHELTERED WITH THE JERK

AMARYLLIS LANZA

Published by Blushing Books
An Imprint of
ABCD Graphics and Design, Inc.
A Virginia Corporation
977 Seminole Trail #233
Charlottesville, VA 22901

Sheltered with the Jerk
By Amaryllis Lanza

EBook ISBN:
978-1-63954-239-0

Chapter 1

I really shouldn't drink mojitos, but I'd give anything for a beer now.

HANGOVERS SUCK. Drinking until you black out is a terrible idea. College life is dangerous enough without losing consciousness and suffering gaps in memory, but partying was what I did best. You can judge me all you like. If you don't enjoy life while you're young, then you wind up with regrets. I'd seen it happen to my mother, and I would not allow it to happen to me. I planned to make the most of my youth and beauty, while I could. *Carpe* fucking *diem.* Right?

That said, I had plenty of regrets when the cold water splashed on my face, waking me out of a pleasant dream about swimming with dolphins.

"The fuck?" I shouted, rising from the couch, my eyes struggling to focus. My head ached like a sledge-hammer had played the chicken dance on repeat, on my skull. "Ow…" I whimpered. My mouth was sticky cotton for a moment, then it filled with bile and last night's mojitos as my stomach woke up too. *Blech.* I threw up before I could stop it, right on the combat boots of the giant asshole who drowned me awake.

"Jesus Christ!" He hopped back, his deep voice booming in my ears like a cannon.

"Shh." I waved my arms, begging him to quiet down, at least while I vomited. *Blech.* I threw up again on the worn rust carpet of—*where was I?* It looked like a small office. The gray tin trashcan my torturer placed between my legs looked like someone had stolen it from a local school. Was he the Principal? I looked up from the boots to the broad, firm, hairy calves and the cut-off fatigues, to an enormous chest wrapped tight under a khaki t-shirt, but then I had to throw up again.

"What time is it?" I asked, still staring at the trashcan, my voice little more than a croak.

"Two."

"In the morning?"

"In the afternoon."

"Why is it so dark?"

"Hurricane shutters are down."

"What?"

"Hurricane. Shutters. Are Down."

"Are you speaking English?" I asked. I couldn't make any sense of what he was saying.

"Who *are* you?" He ignored my question.

"Jenny Banks," I said, then I threw up again. My stomach was mostly empty, but I was retching my liver. This was the downside of the party life. Which party was this? I tried to recall. "And who are *you*?"

"Juan Ruiz." Nope. I didn't know him. Still, I went to lots of strangers' parties. I tried to remember what had happened. It was Friday night, and I went to a club in South Beach, dancing with my girlfriends, then we all got invited to

2

a party somewhere far. I remember driving for a long time to get there. After that, though, things were blurry.

"Where am I?"

"In my fucking house!"

I put my hands over my ears. "Could you *not* do that, please? The shouting. I can't take it. Do you have Alka Seltzer, or a Bloody Mary, or a beer?" I needed serious pain killers or some hair of the dog. "Maybe all three?"

Juan stomped out of the room, loud enough to shatter my eardrums. That's how it felt anyway, despite the carpet. The man walked like a storm trooper.

The small office smelled of vomit—mostly my fault. Soon I was hugging the trashcan again. *Blech.* It was almost all saliva and bile this time, though. I needed fluids.

While my tormentor was gone, I tried to recall more of what had gone on. I was at the club, then the two guys— can't remember their names—invited me to their party. Maggie said I shouldn't drive, but I ignored that, which made me sick to think about. I was lucky not to have died on the road. Though maybe I had died and this was Hell. It sure felt hot enough here.

I did not remember this place at all. I'd followed the guys to a house in the jungle, or something like that. There were lots of trees around, and little else. Then I'd walked around the party for a while—fun crowd, a little rowdy, all college kids like me. Lots and lots of mojitos. Then I felt exhausted and lay down for a while here in the office. It looked different, but I was really drunk so my images of the night were fuzzy.

Stomping intensified as my tormentor returned, shoving a glass of fizzing water in my face.

"Here." Then he threw an old shirt and boxer shorts at me. "Drink that and shower now. You won't be able to shower soon. I need to fill the tub." I just stared at him a while, trying to put those words in some order that made sense. Nope. Fail. "Drink!"

"Please don't shout." I spoke softly, trying to encourage him to do the same.

"Drink."

Okay, I got that part. I drank the glass full of salty, fizzy, head soothing goodness and passed it back to him. He put the glass on the desk and picked me up, along with the shirt and shorts he'd given me. Soon I hung over his shoulder, my head bobbing uncomfortably as we went out of the office, past a large dark den and a darker living room to a flamingo pink hall bathroom. I had protested along the way, but he ignored me and the trip didn't take very long. Juan had long, angry strides.

"I'm going to puke," I said, as soon as he put me down. I knelt at the toilet, but nothing came up immediately. That was fortunate because I needed that Alka Seltzer to do its job.

Juan picked me up off the floor and pulled off my dress. My heels were missing, and I hadn't been wearing a bra, so it was just me and my thong standing there. I wrapped my arms around myself, covering my breasts. There was a lot to cover, but I managed to hide my hard nipples.

"Stop! What are you doing?"

Juan didn't answer. He just lifted me up and placed me in the tub and turned on the freezing water in the shower to rain on my head. "You stink of alcohol," he spat. "Wash up quick, or I'll wash you. You've got five minutes, then I need to fill the tub. Put on the shirt and shorts. Got it?"

"Why do you have to fill the tub?"

"Hank!" His shout reverberated through the pretty pink tiles and pierced my brain like an ice pick.

"No yelling," I said again, waving my hands. Not that he

4

would listen. He was a lunatic. What did that mean? *Hank*? Was that Spanish for something?

He was right, though. I stank. As soon as he left the bathroom, I pulled off my thong and dripped some generic brand shampoo on my head, which hurt just washing it. I rubbed the yellow bar of Dial soap all over myself, which smelled nice. I turned on the hot water because only a madman would wash with cold water. The showerhead rained on me for a while, and I enjoyed the soothing stream, though my scalp complained a bit. All the soap suds were long gone when Juan stormed in again.

"I said, five minutes!" He turned off the water.

"Please," I said. "Do not shout. No yelling. *No es bueno*." I had learned *some* Spanish over the three years I'd been living in Miami, and it seemed like the right time to use it.

He said something under his breath in Spanish I hadn't learned yet, probably something vulgar.

Juan lifted me out of the bathtub—he was a hands-on kind of guy. He turned me against the sink and swatted my naked butt four times really hard. The wet popping sound of his hand striking my bare flesh filled the small bathroom, echoed between my ears, and reverberated through the roots of my teeth. Now my butt hurt as much as my head. Not good.

"Stop!" I shouted. "What are you doing?"

"Waking you up. We've got no time for games, little girl. Get dressed. Hank is coming."

Then Juan knelt to rinse out the tub, put the stopper in, and let the water run to fill it.

"Who the *hell* is Hank?" I rubbed my sore butt and stared at the two logs of well-defined calves on his legs as he waited for the tub to fill.

How dare he spank me? Could I get him to do it again?

"The fucking category five hurricane you almost slept

through!" Juan rose, getting all in my face. Well, his chest, anyway. It was a veritable fortress of a chest, wide and strong, his muscles bulging through the thin khaki fabric of his t-shirt.

"The *what?*"

"Hur-ri-cane."

"As in hurricane?"

Juan shook his head. His shoulder-length wavy dark hair swung from side to side. His dark eyes cut through me and his full lips pressed together in an unforgiving grimace. He was more attractive than most lunatics I'd met, and also a thousand times more scary. Juan said something else in Spanish. I was pretty sure it was a curse word. He pointed at the shirt and boxer shorts laying on the fluffy pink cover of the toilet lid.

"I can't wear that!"

"Fine, be naked." He took the clothes back, but I stopped him before he left.

"No, okay, give me those." I rushed to put them on. "Do you have a spare toothbrush? My mouth tastes awful."

He reached around me to open the mirror vanity and pulled out an extra toothbrush, still in its original package, a tube of Colgate, and a bottle of Listerine. That hard chest was up in my face, right up against my nose. He smelled wonderful, too, like freshly mowed grass and thundershowers. "Hurry. I have to fill the sink. And if you only pee, don't flush the toilet."

"Why?"

"We'll need all the fresh water we can get."

"You're making a big deal out of nothing," I said, dabbing some toothpaste on the toothbrush. "I've been through hurricanes before, you know. NBD."

There had been a few hurricanes since I'd moved to Florida for college. While they meant a lot of rain, and some swinging trees, it was hardly the end of the world. Juan was overreacting, I figured.

"You have not been through one of these," he said. "Nobody in Miami has been through one of these since Andrew."

I looked at him more closely.

"How would you know what Andrew was like?"

I'd heard talk about it, but that was back in 1992. He didn't look that old.

"I was a child, but I will never forget it."

"How old *are* you, then?"

"Old enough to know better. Do what I say, and we'll get through this."

"That's okay, I'll just go home." I shrugged.

Juan shook his head again and sighed. "Too late. You should have left with the rest of the losers I kicked out this morning. All the shutters are up now, and we expect landfall in an hour."

"An *hour*?"

"Yes, brush your teeth, clean the sink and stop it up, then fill it with fresh water. Can you handle that? I've got other preparations to make."

He left before I could answer. "Okay." *Wait.* Was I *stuck* here in *where, exactly?* With this *crazy person*? I needed my phone to call my friends. As soon as I brushed my teeth and gargled a few times with Listerine, I did as Juan asked, cleaning and filling the sink. Then I went back to the office to look for my purse. I found Juan in there, on his knees, washing my vomit off the carpet with some kind of cleaning powder and a scrub brush. He was cursing a blue streak in Spanish. He had a very nice, tight ass, a really strong back, and giant arms. I had no business noticing that, but it was hard to miss.

"Where's my purse?" I asked, looking around.

"How would I know?" he barked.

"Please. The yelling. We talked about this. Remember?"

"It's not my fault if you're a drunk," he said.

"I'm not a drunk."

"Really? You sure act like one. What kind of woman drinks so much she passes out in a stranger's house and gets sick all over the place? Don't you have any self-respect?"

"Don't judge me," I said, straightening my back to look down on him. "You don't know me."

"I don't *want* to know you," he said. "But I'm stuck with you for now."

"Tell me where my purse is. I need my phone to call my friends."

"Why would I know where your purse is?" He really wasn't even trying to lower his volume. I winced. "I didn't even know you were *here*. All your friends left without you early this morning. I'd say they aren't excellent friends."

"Again, with the shouting and the judging."

"Shut up." Juan stood up. "Do me a favor—just sit in the living room and stay out of my way. I've got things to do. More things than I had planned because of you."

"If you tell me what you need, I could help." I wanted to prove him wrong. Not sure why that mattered, except I didn't want him feeling all superior.

"Actually, you know how to boil water, right?"

"Duh." I made a face. "I can cook too. What do you need?"

"I need you to go to the kitchen, fill every pot and boil water in it."

"Seriously?"

"Yes."

"I think you're going overboard."

"Just do it, or don't."

"Fine." I raised my palms. "Where's the kitchen?"

8

"You passed it on your way here. It's to your left when you get out," he said. "While you're in there, drink as much water as you can handle. You're going to need extra hydration to get through this in your state."

"What I need is a beer," I grumbled, mostly to myself, but he heard me.

"There's no alcohol in the house," he said. "I tossed out what hadn't already been drunk."

"What a waste."

"Just go, Jenny Banks." He slapped my butt again.

"Ouch! Do you spank all the women you meet?"

"Yes, especially the ones who deserve it."

Okay, I was stuck going through hurricane Hank with a grump who loved spanking me.

This should be fun.

Chapter 2

It's all bad news from here on.

AFTER I HAD BOILED ALL the water and drunk as much as I could, I sat in the living room to watch the television. It was a smaller room than the den, at the back of the house, but the den had sliding glass doors, which Juan had sealed off with metal shutters. He figured the living room, which was at the center of the house, was the safest place for us to wait for Hank to arrive.

Juan had tuned-in to the local news station for updates. The reporters all seemed just about as freaked out about Hank as Juan was. For the first time, I really got scared. After all, I did not know what it would mean to go through a category five hurricane. If the hurricane tracker on Channel 10 was anything to go by, I might as well say my prayers.

I hadn't been able to find my purse anywhere in the house after searching for it, so my friends had no way of knowing whether I was okay or not. I wondered if they were worried about me. Though, to be honest, nobody really ever was, starting with my parents. If I died during this thing, how many weeks would it take for anyone to notice? It made me sad to think about that for too long, and I cried.

Just then, Juan walked into the living room, bringing me another glass of water with Alka Seltzer in it, and a turkey sandwich on white toast. He sat next to me on the large brown sofa.

"Don't cry," he said, gently. "You're safe. We'll be fine."

"I'm not crying."

"What is this, then?" He brushed a tear away from my damp cheek with a rough thumb.

"My head aches and I'm hung over. My eyes sting."

"Okay, Jenny Banks," he said. "Eat your sandwich."

"I'm not hungry."

"Eat the sandwich."

"I'll probably throw it up."

"I won't tell you a third time."

"Jesus, you're bossy!" I complained, but I reached for a wedge and took a careful nibble. The toasted bread made it better, and mercifully there was no mayonnaise in there to unsettle my stomach, only lean turkey meat and Swiss cheese. I took another bite, and another. Soon I'd finished the wedge.

Juan sat quietly watching the news, his jaw clenched hard, which somehow made him more attractive. He was intense, like the hurricane we were expecting.

"So, is this your house, then?" I asked, reaching for the other wedge of sandwich. Now that the first bit had settled, I found I was hungry.

"Whose house would it be?"

"Well, I don't know," I said. "I mean. They invited me to a party, so I assumed it belonged to those guys."

"It didn't. It doesn't. Those guys had no business inviting anyone and they know it."

"So, like, are they your brothers or something?"

Juan snorted, suppressing a bitter laugh. "Or something."

"What does that mean?"

"None of your business," Juan snapped. "The point is, none of you belonged here last night and you all made a mess of my house on the worst possible day."

I shrugged. "Sorry, but I had no way to know."

"I don't blame you for that," Juan said. "But seriously, what is a girl like you thinking following some strangers to a party and then getting so drunk you don't hear it when everyone gets kicked out? Anything could have happened to you, you know. It's not safe!"

I put my sandwich slice back down and swallowed the small bite I had just bitten off. "Hey, stop with the judging. Like I said, you don't know me. And no more yelling, please."

"I have a right to ask," Juan said. "You've created a terrible situation for both of us, and what's coming our way will require you to show some sense."

"I have plenty of sense. I've handled some pretty big things on my own, for longer than you have, probably."

"I doubt it. How old are you, anyway?"

"Twenty-two. But I've been pretty much by myself since I was six. Technically, I've been adulting longer than you."

Juan scoffed at that. "Child, you are not adulting yet. You obviously do not know what the word means. And, it's not a word, by the way. It's made up. It's not grammatical."

"But you understood what I meant, right?"

"That's not the point."

"Whatever."

We listened to the news in silence for a while, watching

the hurricane tracker map play repeatedly, showing the same thing—we were fucked, basically.

"What part of Miami are we in?" I asked, wondering which part of the target we were. Not that it made much difference. Hank looked big enough and mean enough to swallow all of South Florida whole.

"It's not really Miami," he said. "It's South Dade."

"So, like, where is that?"

"South," he said, then he rose to point at the television screen, which showed us right at the heart of the scary red path of Hank. *Great. Just Great.* "Don't you remember where you went last night?"

I had picked up the slice of sandwich again and had to swallow a bite before answering. "Not really. I just remember it was a long drive."

"We're near the zoo." He sat back next to me, which made the sofa feel much smaller again.

"I haven't been to the zoo. I don't like zoos."

"Why?"

"Well, first, it's cruel keeping animals trapped like that where they don't belong, just so people can gawk at them. Second, I don't like zoos."

Juan smiled. "You don't want to tell me why, right?"

"It's none of your business."

"You're right. I don't care. Just so you know, though, I work at the zoo and it's not what you think. They take care of the animals, and there's a lot of excellent research coming out of there."

"What kind of research?"

"They have an entire program on conservation, plus all the animal behavioral research. Lots of stuff."

"Most of the animals don't belong here," I said. "They're trapped where they don't want to be. They belong free in their natural habitats."

"Where some of them might be hunted to extinction," Juan noted.

"I don't know about that." I shrugged. "It's not my field, but in principle they shouldn't be locked up in cages or left wandering through smaller than natural habitats."

"What is your field, then? Fashion? Partying?"

"Child psychology."

Juan laughed a booming laugh, like I'd just made the biggest joke on the planet. *Asshole.*

"What's so funny about that?"

"You think and act like a child, so I guess it fits."

"Look, Mister Judgy Pants, like I said, you don't know me."

"Yeah?" Juan turned on the sofa to look at me like he was seeing me for the first time and wanted to memorize me for a test. "Okay, you have abandonment issues, probably your father. You have no sense of self-preservation, probably low self-esteem, though you act tough about it. You are riddled with self-doubt and overcompensate by acting super confident. You have no real friends because you push people away. You are only comfortable with superficial relationships, so you don't have to feel anything when it falls apart. You want to be a child psychologist because you're trying to fix something you can't fix."

"Fuck you," I spat, stretching and stiffening my spine as straight as I could make it.

"Okay, so I'm right."

"No, you're not. You're just a jerk." I stuck my tongue out at him. "Two can play that game, you know." I tried to scrutinize him the way he had with me. I might not have got the face right, but I could communicate contempt in my own way. "You're a former soldier and suffer from PTSD. Working at the zoo started as a way for you to cope with all that. It's become a crutch. The only time you feel right is when you're caring for the animals, so you're blind to the rest of it. Your family is a mess. You come from a broken home and your stepbrothers don't respect you. You haven't got over army training and you obsess over stupid shit. The world is chaos and you can't handle that, so you insist on putting everything in order. It's like trying to control the tide, though, and you know it. You have no actual relationships because you worry that you'll scare anyone away who dares to care for you. It's easier to be an antisocial loner than a monster in the eyes of someone you might love."

I felt smart for about a minute, then the look on his face made me sick. I'd hit a nerve and regretted it instantly.

"I'm sorry." I reached out to touch his thigh. "I can be a bitch sometimes."

"We need lamps." He rose from the sofa and left me alone.

What the fuck was wrong with me? I had to wonder. After all, the man had helped me in his own way. He could have just tossed me out on the street and wished me luck with the hurricane. I mean, he had shuttered up the house, but he could have opened one shutter just to let me get to my car. Now, I wouldn't make it anywhere in time. That's probably where my purse was, I thought suddenly. In my car. It made sense that I wouldn't have wanted to carry it with me, though leaving my keys in the car would have been stupid, assuming I did that. Juan was right. I had no business drinking until I blacked out, but there was a lot he was wrong about.

I mean, my father hadn't exactly abandoned me at the zoo. He had a nervous breakdown while taking me to the zoo and disappeared. As a result, I was lost a long while on my own. My mother had not coped well with my father being stuck in a constant loop going in and out of an asylum, getting better, then getting worse again. She wasn't an exceptional mother to begin with, but she got worse. I had to fend for myself if I wanted to eat, or dress, or whatever. I figured it out just fine, though, after a while. Fortunately, we had a house that was paid for and more than enough money in the bank that my mother drinking herself into a stupor every day made no difference. We weren't tossed into the streets. But I had to be an adult long before Juan probably did, in relative time. So, if I wanted to act like a child for a while, that was my prerogative. To me, it only made sense to seize the day. Anything can happen. Anytime. You don't want to be full of nothing but regrets when it does.

I stared at the news for a while, thinking none of it seemed real. Maybe the hurricane would miss us at the last minute. It could happen. Maybe. I needed a drink. Juan came by after a while of running around the house, making more preparations. I figured out what he meant by lamps when he put a battery-powered hurricane lamp and a transistor radio on the large, square, wood coffee table in the living room, in front of the couch. He also brought two Publix bags full of water bottles and snacks.

"This is the second most isolated room in the house, so we'll be staying here, mostly," he said. "If things get worse, we'll rush to the office, which has better protection because of the foundation wall and it's up against the garage. I figured we'll want to have more room between us while we ride it out, though."

He was right. The office would be cramped with both of us in it, not to mention the smell which, again, was mostly my fault. I hoped we wouldn't have to go there overnight.

"Tell me about hurricane Andrew." If he was just going to pretend that what I'd said to upset him earlier hadn't happened, I was totally cool with that. It was for the best.

"I'd rather not talk about that right now. Just follow what I ask you to do, okay?"

"Why?"

"What?"

"Why don't you want to talk about Andrew? It's relevant, don't you think?"

Juan shook his head. "No two hurricanes are alike. All you need to know is that there is nothing you can do but hold on tight and pray at this point. I've built this house to take it, but even the best construction can fail against nature's wrath."

"*You* built this house?"

"Mostly, yes. I had some help."

"It looks like they designed it in the seventies or something."

"It's built exactly like my old house," Juan explained. "The one that used to be here, but this one is much stronger."

"What happened to the other one?" I asked, though I already knew the answer even as I asked. "Did Andrew wipe out your old house with you in it?"

Juan didn't have to answer. His dark expression said everything. Shit, a little kid going through something like that. It would have been awful.

"Were you okay?"

"I'm here, aren't I?"

"Yeah, but…"

"But nothing. The key is to survive, whatever comes."

Juan certainly came across as a survivor and a fighter. He looked like he could be a pro-wrestler, to be honest, all lean, bulging muscle. He could probably punch the hurricane away. Or just scare it off with a stare, like the one he was giving me that minute. I looked away and finished my sandwich.

"Thank you for helping me," I said, after swallowing the last bite. "You didn't have to do that."

"You didn't leave me a choice."

"Well, you could have just kicked me out."

"Don't be ridiculous," he said. "You'd die out there on the road."

"I'm not completely helpless, you know. I can be useful in a crisis."

"Yeah? Well, we'll know soon enough."

I was in a sour mood, and the news wasn't helping. They had reporters standing on the beach pointing at waves. Some surfers had decided the hurricane was the perfect opportunity to die a glorious death. Idiots.

"Do we have to keep watching this? I mean, I get it. It's bad. But could we watch something else?"

"Like what?" He stroked my hair, which was a little tangled. It hadn't dried right.

"I don't know. Do you have the Disney channel?"

Juan chuckled, but he picked up the remote control and put on the channel, anyway. "You may as well enjoy it while it lasts." It was part way through *Beauty and the Beast*, right at the library scene, which instantly cheered me up.

"Thank you." I curled up to watch, tucking my legs under myself.

"You're welcome." Juan relaxed too, leaning back on the couch, with his hands clasped behind his head, putting his long legs up on the coffee table. The man had enormous feet, I noticed. Like, it must be hard for him to find shoes, which was probably why he still wore his army boots.

"I'm sorry I was mean," I said, meekly, after a long, pleasant silence, during which we both just enjoyed Belle's adventure, as if the world wasn't about to collapse around us. "You deserve better."

"Me too." Juan sounded like he meant it. Maybe he wasn't completely irredeemable, though he *had* spanked me, which was all kinds of inappropriate. But I had really enjoyed it, and couldn't stop wondering whether he might do it again soon.

I didn't feel unsafe around Juan. In fact, I couldn't remember a time when I felt more at ease. I think it was just his cool confidence, because otherwise it made little sense. I didn't know this man at all and we were in danger. But he'd given me shelter, made me a sandwich, and didn't mind watching a cartoon musical with me instead of the news. That had to count for something. Juan could be mean, but he was also nicer than most guys I knew. Admittedly, I didn't really know a lot of great guys. Not that the guys I knew were bad, but they were just party people, somewhat selfish and very immature. Juan wasn't a guy. I mean, he was a man. He had his shit together. Maybe he was a bit of a grouse, and somewhat twisted—and a spanker—but I had the sense that under all that gruffness, he was an honorable man.

I relaxed, leaning up against him on the couch, and he didn't push me away. Instead, Juan rested his hand on my shoulder. It felt warm there. Solid. It felt wonderful.

Of course, that had to be when the power went out because that's how shit goes.

"It's here," Juan announced, as a loud low rumble sounded just outside, like a high-speed train. That was the beginning of the end.

And the end of the beginning.

Chapter 3

We're riding the railway to heaven, and I want to get off.

I ACTUALLY GREW up around trains. My family was in the rail industry originally. My dad had loved to play with trains when he was small, and he had set up a huge model of our city—Reading, Pennsylvania—with a complete rail system looping around it in his private office. I would spend hours marveling at the train going round when I was little. That's before Dad had his big, bad breakdown. Then we just sort of avoided that part of the house and let the spiders have it. I went back in there, just before I left home for college, and even with layers of dust and spider webs everywhere, the model still worked. It was beautiful, and it made me feel sad Dad didn't play with his train anymore.

Hank was a different sort of train, though just as persistent. It got louder and louder and kept whistling and howling and rumbling for hours. It made my headache much worse. Each time a loose branch or palm frond crashed against the metal barrier of the shutters, I jumped. At one point, it sounded like an entire tree slammed up against us, and I screamed. Juan pulled me close, wrapping me in his arms, which felt great. I'm not sure whether he was trying to comfort me or use me as his stuffie, but I honestly didn't care either way.

"Don't worry, little one," he said. "The house will hold."

"How can you be sure? You can't be sure."

"Trust me." He stroked my hair. "The shutters are strong and the roof is reinforced. The walls are solid. Nothing will blow this house apart a second time."

"Hank sounds like he really wants to."

"That's just nature making a point."

"What point?"

"All we are is dust in the wind."

"I don't like that song," I muttered. My mom would play it often and I fucking hated it, to be honest.

"What kind of music do you like?" Juan was obviously trying to distract me from my panic. It wasn't working, but I played along for a while. Sometimes, if you pretend to feel a certain way long enough, the feeling sticks.

"I don't know, dance music, I guess. Happy songs. I like nothing too deep and I don't like how some songs try to make you cry."

Juan kept running his fingers through my hair, tucking a curl behind my ear. My hair had probably dried funny. It is mostly a springy, frizzy mess of brown curls when I don't do something about it. It has no discipline at all, left on its own. Juan hadn't really left me much time to groom myself, and with my purse missing, I couldn't, anyway. I was sure I looked pretty awful, which was why it was so weird when he suddenly kissed me.

It was a gentle kiss, almost as if he wasn't sure he should do that. I guess, since we were both strangers stuck together by chance, he had a valid reason to feel insecure. But I wasn't. I was totally ravenously horny for him. I mean, he was a very sexy man—tan, tall, muscular with longish dark hair and stubble—just my type, except for the whole being an asshole thing. But I could work with that.

The situation seemed to call for a distraction. So I kissed him back, encouraging him, and transferred myself to straddle his lap, wrapping my arms over those broad shoulders and digging my nails into his strong back as I drank him up.

"Stop," he said, pulling back, though he didn't pull me off his lap and his hands were both gripping my ass pretty tight. "We can't do this."

"Why?"

"Because we don't know each other," he said. "Do you just sleep with men you don't know at all?"

"I don't want to sleep with you," I said. "I want to fuck you. That's different."

"No," he said, and this time took me off his lap, which made me miss the massive hard-on I had been so pleasantly pressed against. "I'm too old for you."

"No, you're not," I said, kneeling on the couch next to him and giving him a sour face.

"You're too young for me," he said. "And you wouldn't want what I'm into, anyway."

"Try me," I straddled him again. "I might surprise you."

"Stop, Jenny Banks," he said, pushing my hips away from his hardness.

"Why do you do that?"

"I told you. It's wrong for us to do this."

"No, I mean, why do you call me by my full name? It's weird. You can just call me Jenny."

"No," he said. "That's too much like we're friends, and we're not. We're strangers."

I sat back on his lap and crossed my arms. "Look, why are you being such a jerk about this? You kissed me first."

"You're right," he said. "I shouldn't have started it. Now is a terrible time to do something stupid and impulsive."

I draped my arms over his broad shoulders and gave him a sweet smile as I pressed myself back up against the bar of hot steel trapped under his fatigues. "But you *want* to do something stupid and impulsive, and so do I. We're both grown adults. What's wrong with that?"

"You're much too young for me, Jenny Banks."

"I'm not a girl, and I'm not a virgin. I'm a twenty-two-year-old woman, and I am very turned on right now, and more than willing to fuck your brains out."

"You're not my type," he said, pushing my hips back again.

I jumped off his lap and rushed out of the living room, unsure of where to head. The living room might be the safest room in the house for us to wait out the storm, as he said, because it was actually at the heart of the house, buffered from the windows and doors, in case the shutters gave up the fight. But I didn't want to be in there anymore. I didn't want to be in the house at all. I went to the kitchen, which was also sandwiched between the dining room and the den. It had a window over the sink, but that had shutters over it. Still, it was full of pots of boiled water and there was nowhere for me to sit, except on the cold, amber, ceramic tiles.

So, I left the kitchen and went down the hall to the hall bathroom and locked myself in, sitting on the padded toilet lid, covered with a pink, fluffy cover. It was a very feminine sort of bathroom, I noticed, now that my head was throbbing less and my eyes could focus better than the last time I was in there. A strange choice of decor for a man like Juan, though maybe he literally tried to re-create the house as it had been when he was little. Odd, really, for anyone to do that. I couldn't imagine loving my childhood home so much that I'd want to build another one just like it.

But Juan was weird. What kind of man decides not to fuck you, even though obviously he wants to fuck you very much? And what did he mean by saying I wasn't his type? I was everybody's type. I was usually the one turning guys down. I'm not vain or stuck up, but I know I have a sexy figure and a pretty face. Most days, anyway.

I got up to get a better look at myself in the mirror. Though I only had the blue light of the battery-operated hurricane lamp to see with, I definitely needed make-up. I looked around eighteen without it. Maybe that's what had freaked him out. Well, there was nothing I could do about that without my purse. Plus, my hair really was a mess. I tried combing my fingers through it and searched the bathroom for some hair gel or mousse. Anything that didn't make me look like an underage mess. Juan only had the basic supplies. Whatever. We were probably going to die anyway, going by the constant noise of the train rushing just outside the bath-room window.

What bothered me most, though, was that he implied I was a slut. I wasn't. I had been with a few guys and I liked to party, but I was selective. I didn't offer myself to guys I'd just met. In fact, I never offered myself. Most times, I was fighting guys off. He was the exception. I'd just been feeling vulnerable, and it felt so nice being held, and comforted, and called "little one." It sparked something deep inside me, something I really wanted and I'd never had from any of the guys I'd dated. He had touched the part of me that longed for that kind of relationship—a hard man who might be scary and mean sometimes, but who would also take care of me. I'd fallen into a trap with Juan, succumbing to that need, and then he'd cruelly shoved me away.

Juan was a horrible human being, I decided. As soon as

this damned hurricane passed, I was out of there. How long would that be? Too long, going by the deafening noise of that incessant train. I sat back down on the toilet, covered my ears and cried.

A knock on the door startled me. "Open up, Jenny Banks."

"I'm busy in here."

"You've been in there too long. It's not safe. Finish peeing or whatever you're doing and get back into the living room. We need to talk."

"I have nothing to say to you ever again, Juan Ruiz." If he insisted on being formal, calling me by my full name, I could do it too.

"Now is not the time to throw a tantrum, little girl," he said, sounding stern. "If you're not out of there in five minutes, I'm going to light your ass on fire. Consider yourself forewarned."

"Is that how you solve everything, by spanking the women you're with?"

"Yes," he said, like it was no big deal. Then I heard those boots storm away. What was the point of the carpet in this house? Those enormous feet pounded the ground, regardless. The man was like an un-jolly green giant.

Still, I sat on the toilet a while longer, thinking about how long I'd have to be in there before I'd earn a spanking. He'd said five minutes. But did he have a stopwatch or an internal clock that told him when time was up? Was he serious? Well, he had spanked me without warning earlier. That spanking kept playing in my head, making me hot and wet. Wearing his boxer shorts made that awkward since the crotch hung low and I felt all slippery and exposed. Why was I so horny? Was this just a normal reaction to imminent death?

I had my answer when three things happened almost simultaneously.

First, the metal shutter which had protected the small bathroom window above the tub peeled right off with a loud creaky clank like the hull of the Titanic hitting that iceberg. Then, a loose branch shot through the window like a wooden missile, raining shattered glass bits and splinters of wood everywhere. I screamed as the debris landed on me. The strong wind blowing through the broken window wasn't helping. Almost immediately, Juan kicked the bathroom door off its hinges and carried me out of the bathroom, cursing loudly in Spanish.

I braced myself for a hell of a spanking. Instead, he dropped me on the living room couch and went back down the hall carrying a toolkit that he picked up from the corner of the living room, then produced enough hammering and drilling to reawaken my throbbing headache. I picked the last bits of debris out of my hair, hoping I got all of it. Fortunately, the bathroom window was tempered glass, and it had broken into a crumbly dust instead of shards. I might have been seriously hurt. I went to the kitchen to get a glass of water and search for some Tylenol, but there was nothing like that in there. What I found, in the back of the dark fridge, was a six-pack of beer.

Sneaky son of a…

I popped the top off a bottle of Sol with my back teeth and gulped down the chilly goodness in one long swallow. I didn't get to finish because a monster hand grabbed the bottle right out of mine.

I squeaked and spurted a sip of beer but didn't get to complain before he pressed me up against the sink with the boxer shorts pulled down to my knees. Juan had grabbed a wood spoon out of a drawer and he started whacking my butt with it mercilessly.

"Ow-ow! Stop!" I screeched each time the spoon contacted my flesh.

Juan kept going and going, swatting my ass and my upper thighs, even when I kicked back. He whacked until my ass felt like I'd fallen on ice while skating. It was a deep ache, and part of my butt was numb from the pain, but the part that still felt anything was deeply sore and hot. My rear hurt much worse than my head, worse than anything I'd felt in my life up to that point. I burst into tears and switched to pleading with him to stop, hoping that would work better than shouting insults at him. Eventually, Juan stopped, but he still had me pressed over the sink. There was a tense moment when I could feel his warm erection pressed against my throbbing rear. I thought he might just have to slip inside me then and fuck me raw. I hoped he would—I was so shamefully slick with desire. He had to notice as he used his hand to stroke my injured back cheeks. Juan breathed heavily against my tousled hair. "You... are... a very... *bad...* girl." His voice was a low, hungry growl, which only intensified my dripping need. I raised my rear so his fingers might slip into my slit, where they were desperately wanted. Instead, Juan stepped back, pulled up the boxer shorts and let me go. I felt cold. My rear was ablaze, but my spine missed his warmth.

"Go, Jenny Banks," he said when I finally straightened up again. "Stay out of my way and don't find trouble."

I thought Juan would follow me to the living room, but he didn't.

Sitting wasn't an option anymore, so I just stood staring at the glowing blue light of the hurricane lamp, playing that scene over and over in my head, wondering what the fuck I just got myself into and how soon I might get Juan riled up enough to pull his spoon out again.

Maybe next time, he'd finish what he started.

Chapter 4

I'm going to die with nothing but a hangover and a sore butt.

I COULD HEAR Juan stomping around the rest of the house, still trying to fix whatever he could in the bathroom. I couldn't budge to lend a hand. I ached so badly, worse than before, not so much from the spanking but from the unsatisfied lust it had raised in me. I could still hear his growl echoing in my mind. *"You… are… a very… bad… girl."*

Okay, but was I *his* very bad girl now or just a generic very bad girl? I needed to know.

As time went by, I worried Juan might regret what he had done to me. Because it had been raw and in some ways awful, but it also felt fantastic. Was he really fixing things or just avoiding me now? I needed to find out.

I left the living room, taking the hurricane lamp with me, and went to see what he was up to in the hallway. As I passed the hall bathroom, I noticed the howling wind had stopped whipping around. Juan had somehow secured the window with a plank of plywood fitted into the space. There were some sort of metal clips holding it firm. It looked like it might hold, at least for a while. Juan must have pre-cut covers for all the windows, I figured, because I hadn't heard a buzz-saw.

He'd really thought this whole hurricane thing through, expecting the worst to happen. Juan was a man who liked to be prepared, who appreciated order, yet he'd done something impulsive and chaotic with me. Spanking me with a spoon, then rubbing my rear to soothe the ache was completely inappropriate, even if it left me slippery and craving more of his hard hand.

Maybe he regretted it. Well, I sure as shit did not.

The broken branch which had flown through the window lay on the floor tiles, to the side, under the towel rack. Splinters of wood from that floated on the surface of the full tub like lost ships at sea. I fished them out with my hand and threw them into the small white wicker trash basket, doing the same in the sink. Glass bits gathered at the bottom, shining under the light of the hurricane lamp like pebbles in a lonely fishbowl. I figured it was best to leave those where they were. This wouldn't be drinking water for us, anyway. It occurred to me I had been very lucky to be sitting on the toilet crying. If it had happened five seconds earlier, while I stood at the sink, looking at myself in the mirror, the branch would have hit me.

Juan had put the door back, which he'd had to kick down too. I felt foolish for locking him out, making extra work for him, but I had needed some time to myself. He should understand that.

Clearly, he also needed some time to himself because Juan was missing.

I left the bathroom, closing the door just in case the new plywood cover on the window failed, and walked down the hallway to check the other rooms. There were three bedrooms in all. Two smaller ones on either side of the hall, just past the bathroom. Juan wasn't in either of those. The rooms were dark, but with the light of the lamp, I could see that Juan had neatly appointed them with tidy pale wood furnishings and single beds. He might be in the master bedroom at the end of the hall, I figured, so I knocked tentatively on the door and waited. When I didn't get an answer, I tried the knob, and opened the door slowly, then stepped inside.

Juan sat at the foot of a king-sized bed at the back of the room with his head in his hands.

"Hey," I said, coming up to him. "Are you okay?"

"You shouldn't be here," he said, not looking up.

"I know, but I'm sort of stuck now. Can we talk about…"

He looked up and gave me a fierce expression. "No."

"I really need to talk about it."

Juan shook his head. "I shouldn't have done that to you. You're… Fuck!"

"I liked it," I said, putting my hand gently on his shoulder. He looked at me like I was crazy—which, maybe I was. "I needed it. Thank you. I would have liked it better if you had made me come."

"You didn't earn that," he said.

I smiled at him. "Okay, I can see that. I was a very bad girl. You were mean, though, and you lied to me about the beer."

"You shouldn't be drinking in the middle of a hurricane! It's irresponsible. You drink too much and it leads to bad things." He gave me a hard look and the shadows from the lamp made his sharp features even more menacing. He was like a panther waiting to strike. Then he took a deep breath and transferred his annoyance back to himself. "I had no business doing that. I don't know you. You make me crazy… But that's no excuse. We can't take this any further."

"I think you're wrong. What else is there to do? I get the rule about no drinking, I guess. We want to make sober decisions. But sex might be wonderful." I ran my fingers through his dark hair and found it much softer than I had expected. It made me a little jealous. My hair needed a lot of products before it ever felt as silky as that. "Sex could help us work off some of the tension, don't you think?"

"No, I'm more tense now than I was before." He brushed my hand away. "I can't trust myself around you. You're too young and you're going to be here for who knows how long."

"Be honest now," I said, reaching for him again, caressing his stubbly chin. "Did you enjoy spanking me?"

"Yes, I enjoyed it," he said, reaching around to stroke my butt. "I just don't know how you could."

"Well, I didn't really enjoy the spanking so much," I said, pouting. "No, that's a lie. I enjoyed the spanking too. You *know* I did. No one's ever done that to me before and it's something I've always wanted. It's something I've needed, and I didn't know how to ask for it. The men I've been with haven't really had what it takes."

He looked up at me again, this time with a wry grin and a furrow on his brow.

"How many men *have* you been with?"

"Only a handful," I said. "I'm not really a slut, you know. Maybe I'm an alcoholic, but I don't think so. I just… Look, it's complicated. I *am* a bad girl, though. Do you think you can turn me into a good girl, at least for a little while? I think I enjoy being bad, but I'd be good for the right hard-handed man."

"Is that really what you want?" he asked.

"Yes," I said. "I want a man to sort me out, lay down the law, punish me when I'm naughty. Are you available?"

He shook his head again and let go of my ass. I missed his hand there. "No, Jenny Banks, you're too young."

"Stop saying that! I'm not a child. I'm a grown woman."

"But I'm thirty-seven, Jenny Banks. I might not be old enough to be your father, but damned close."

"So, why are you single?"

"It's complicated."

"No, it's not." I stroked his hair again. "You haven't found someone who likes what you like, who wants what you want. I want to be handled the way only you could handle me—all rough and demanding. And I'm *completely* available."

"Stop," he said, getting up, so he towered over me. His broad chest was in my face, right up against my nose, and I had trouble looking away. I took a deep breath to soak in that scent of mint and grass, melded now with something amber and salty. I wanted to pull off his shirt and lick him. Maybe he'd taste like saltwater taffy. "Stop making trouble and stop making assumptions. And *especially* stop being so *damned horny*. There's a hurricane out there, for heaven's sake. Can't you hear it?"

"Right now, the only thing I can hear is the thumping of my heart," I said, barely above a breathy whisper.

It was true, though part of it was just my head and my butt throbbing, for different reasons, and the other part was the pulsing of my pussy and the rushing of my blood through my eardrums, plus the crackling static of his proximity. But whatever. The point is there was a lot of noise in my body. He was the reason for most of it.

"Fuck," he said, softly caressing my cheek, tipping my chin up to look into those dark eyes. I practically fell up into them. They sucked me up like the vacuum of space, and soon I was on tip-toe reaching for his full lips.

"Please." I barely breathed the word. There was no breath left in my body.

"We're going to regret this," he said, speaking against my lips as he took my face in his hands.

"Not if the hurricane kills us," I said. "Then, at least we will have both died properly fucked."

"Bad girl," he growled, but his twisted grin took the edge off. Then he lifted me up by the ass, as if I were nothing but a doll for him to play with, and I hooked my arms around his broad shoulders and wrapped my legs around his midriff. He kissed me like he was trying to take his revenge on my mouth. I melted under his tongue like shaved ice and let him drink me whole.

It would have been glorious sex, I'm sure. We were both more than ready for it.

As Juan turned to drop me on the black silk sheets, we heard the roaring of the train intensify. Then there was an unholy crack, as if the bow of Noah's ark had hit a mountaintop. The low, raspy groan of an enraged titan followed. Juan ran out of the bedroom, still carrying me like a monkey hooked around his neck, while the roof flew right off the spot where we were just a moment earlier. He placed me under the dining room table and barked at me to stay put, not that I planned to go anywhere. I was terrified. He went back down the hall, which in my mind made him some kind of lunatic. He came back carrying two large bags in each hand and dropped two of them at my feet under the table. I looked inside and found water bottles and snacks, and a hurricane lamp and a wind-up transistor radio. While I checked these out, he unzipped one bag, releasing a compressed roll-up mattress which he zip-tied to the legs on the long side of the table. He came to the other side of the table to do the same with a second mattress, so I sat in a semi-fortress made of table and mattress—a bizarre situation I could barely wrap my mind around.

Then Juan knelt under the table through the narrow opening to explain.

"For flying debris," he said. "It's not much, but it's better than nothing. Stay put."

He disappeared again for a while and came back armed with styrofoam panels and a large stapler, stapling the narrow end of the table behind me closed. Then he came into the fortress with me, with his back covering the opening.

"We're going to die, aren't we?" I asked, as soon as he had stopped breathing hard.

"No, this is still not so bad."

"Are you *kidding*? The roof just came off!"

"Only over the master bedroom," he said. "The rest of the house is holding for now."

"What is *this* supposed to accomplish?" I asked, raising my hands at my sides to point at what felt like a little play-time fortress.

"It's how I survived Andrew," he said. "I was under the table when the house blew away. Things fell on the table, but not on me. I added the mattresses as cushions, just in case. It'll work."

"Your entire house blew away, and you were stuck under a table when you were a little kid?"

"Yes," he said.

I tried to imagine Juan as a little boy, but he was so big that it was hard to picture him ever being anything else. Still, for a child, going through that, it must have been awful. It would have been traumatic in a way which can mark you for life. Some of Juan's almost obsessive preparations made sense. I only wondered why he'd bothered to stay in Florida when he could live anywhere, and why he'd insisted on rebuilding the house Andrew destroyed.

"And your parents?"

"My mom survived," he said. "She landed on their mattress—injured—but it did not kill her."

"What about your dad?"

Juan shook his head. "A flying beam struck him."

"I'm sorry." I put my hand on his knee. "It must have been horrible."

"That was the simple part. The horror follows."

I don't think he was trying to terrify me, but it worked anyway. Why couldn't I have stayed in Pennsylvania? They had superb colleges and the worst thing that could happen to me there would be getting stuck in a blizzard. I knew how to survive those.

"I hate hurricanes." I didn't mean to cry again, but I couldn't stop myself.

Juan pulled me to sit nestled between his legs, protected by his broad body, wrapped in his brawny arms.

"Nothing is going to hurt you, baby." He kissed the top of my head, which soothed me a little. "We're going to make it."

I wanted to believe him, but it sure seemed hard to accept with the howling growing all around us and the chug-chugging of the Hank train, and the cracking as the roof split closer to where we sat.

"This is hell," I wept. "Now, we won't even get to do it and I was really looking forward to that. I'm going to die with nothing but a hangover and a sore butt. I hate Miami."

"You will *not* die," Juan promised, squeezing me tight. "And it's for the best that we had to stop. When the storm passes, we'll see if you still want me. If you do, then we'll talk."

Juan reached around me to grab the transistor radio and we listened to the news reports in silence, praying that the rest of the roof would hold.

Chapter 5

Welcome to the Hank-pocalypse.

MAYBE IT WAS the dull drone of the reporter's voice on the transistor radio, sharing the same useless bits of information repeatedly on a loop. There were only a few terrifying updates here and there where they could get reporters on scene, major roads inaccessible, trailer trucks overturned on the highway, million dollar yachts stacked on rooftops of multi-million dollar homes. Miami was broken —all of South Florida was—torn to shreds and some of it drowning. But the cracking had stopped above us and it seemed the rest of the roof held tight. Or maybe I just got used to the howling wind all around us, the chug-chug-chugging of Hank's hungry engine. Maybe it was the bit of beer I'd drunk, or the way Juan had warmed my bottom for me. Maybe it was because Juan was my firm and safe ground. He held me, cuddled against his body like he would never let me go. Even if a tornado scooped us up and tossed us clear to Oz, he would be the solid house I landed on.

Whatever it was, at some point, I gave in to sleep.

I woke up alone, lying on the large fluffy brown couch in the den, under a crocheted quilt of colorful grandma squares. The sun in my eyes was much too bright. Though I'd only had less than half a beer, I felt worse than hung-over. I felt like I'd been chewed up by a monster and thrown up again in the apocalypse. My eyes took in my surroundings as I sat up. Juan had obviously removed the shutters from the sliding glass doors in the den, which explained the blinding light, and there was a roof over my head which meant at least the back part of the house had held up. I got up and wandered to the middle of the house. The living room was intact, just as Juan had predicted. As I walked to the end, I saw the kitchen and the dining room held too, which was great news. Even our little improvised dining table and mattress fortress were still there, though Juan wasn't.

When I turned to the right, though, there was nothing but debris. The entry way to the house had blown clear off. Juan had a new front porch, which was basically the slab of the house's foundation. The hallway which led to the guest bath and bedrooms was still there, but cluttered with broken things. I called out Juan's name a few times. When I didn't hear him answer back, I stepped forward, carefully, to avoid the fallen plaster, broken roof tiles, and the rest of the mess. I hopped through the visible spots of carpet, which were squishy under my feet on landing. It was saturated with rain and would definitely need to be replaced, but that seemed like the least of the problems with Juan's house at this point. I called out for Juan again, looking up at the exposed beams of roof through gaps on the ceiling. It wasn't an orderly tear. It was as if something had crashed through the roof, maybe a tractor trailer, given what the news had been reporting before

I zonked out. Maybe a flying yacht. Anything was possible in this sunny hell scape.

That struck me as ironic, how very blue the sky was, how pure the air felt around me. It was as if Hank had wiped a slate clean on the planet, and we were just the chalk dust left behind. Was that what hurricanes were for? To clear the air? Or were they meant to remind us we were tiny and very frail and nature was a huge, unforgiving, angry bitch?

"What the fuck are you doing, woman?" The deep voice startled me out of my wandering thoughts, as did the giant hopping down from the roof right onto the layer of plaster and debris below, his enormous boots landing like Thor's hammer on the broken ground. "You're barefoot! Get back to the den this minute."

"I just wanted to see if I could help."

"Yes, you can help by not getting tetanus, for fuck's sake. I don't need you injured on top of everything else. Plus, there are loose wires. You'd get electrocuted if the power came back on."

I hopped back the way I came, and he followed with large strides, making a loud stomping noise behind me. I felt like Jack being chased down the beanstalk, but I was determined not to let Juan intimidate me.

"You should have woken me up," I said, standing by the entrance to the kitchen, which looked better and brighter now that the shutter was off the window over the sink. "I could have done something."

"There's plenty for you to do," he said. "Enough work to keep you busy for days, but you needed your sleep. Besides, I had things to do, and you'd only have been in the way. We've got to improvise some shoes for you. Maybe my beach shoes would work."

"I don't know. Your feet are pretty long and wide."

"Well, you can't go around barefoot. It's not safe."

"I have my gym bag in the car," I said. "I think my purse and keys are in there, too. It's probably open."

"What car?"

"*My* car," I said.

"You *drove* here?"

"Yeah."

"Were you *sober*?"

"Mostly," I said, unable to meet his eyes. "Yes."

Juan huffed, putting his fists on his hips. He didn't believe me for a minute, but now was not the time to argue about my poor decisions on the night of the party. "Where did you park, then?"

"I don't really remember. Outside somewhere. There were a bunch of cars around the house, so I had to walk, but it wasn't too far. Maybe half a block."

"There's nothing left on the block," Juan said. "Definitely no cars. There's only my jeep because it's in the garage—which held up."

"Are you saying my car blew away?"

"Or someone stole it during the party. Why would you leave your keys and your purse outside in the car?"

"So I wouldn't lose them at the party, obviously."

Juan shook his head at me. "You need minding."

I smiled up at his sexy angry face and drew my nail down his bare, glistening chest. "I know. Are you available?"

He grabbed my wrist to stop me from going further down. "You don't know what you're asking for, Jenny Banks. Besides, we've got too much to do right now, just to stay alive. I don't have time to play house with a brat."

I pouted. "You promised we'd talk about it after the hurricane."

"Yes, I did, but not right away. I've got to finish covering the roof with a tarp. Right now, there's no rain, but there will be. The sun shining on us won't be great either. I've got to clear out all this debris and close the entrance to the house again. There may be looters coming over the next few days. We can't be vulnerable out in the open."

"So what do I do?"

"I need to find you some shoes and some other clothes to wear," he noted. "For now, just sit on the couch and behave."

"I can't just sit on my ass while you do everything. That's not the way I work."

"Fair enough, but give me a chance to find you something to cover your feet and your little ass."

"The shorts work fine, though they are a little dirty," I said, flashing lashes at him. "That's your fault for making me all wet and leaving me wanting."

"Just sit, Jenny," he said, and the fact he didn't add my last name made me smile more.

"Yes, sir," I said, standing on tiptoes to give him a peck on the chin before I turned to comply. He pulled me up for a quick kiss, then he smacked my ass pretty hard. I hopped away, feeling much better than I had in days. Months maybe. Years.

I felt victorious, which was really getting ahead of myself, but that's what's wrong with me.

───────

Juan was gone for a long while, trying to find me footwear. I suppose the master bedroom was a mess, just from what I could see down the hall. I hoped he could find something that wasn't wet or damaged. It really was inconvenient being basically naked and barefoot after an event like this. I had been totally unprepared. Fortunately, Juan was Mr. Preparedness. When the end of the world came, he said, 'Bring it on.'

He came back to the den with a pair of beach shoes, which had solid rubber bottoms with thick treads and a mesh top. They were way too big for me and looked like clown shoes on my feet, but they had high enough tops that the mesh held around my ankles. After a while, I got used to waddling in them without tripping too badly. He also brought me a spare white t-shirt and draw-string bathing suit shorts, with a palm tree print, that were long enough on me to pass for decent, if extremely unfashionable, Bermuda shorts. They had pockets, which was useful, and a mesh liner which unfortunately was more uncomfortable against my skin than his soft cotton boxer shorts. I wasn't about to complain. Juan wasn't in the mood to hear me whine about clothing. Something had happened while he was searching in the bedroom. I wondered what.

"Is everything okay?" I asked.

"It'll be fine," he said, tossing me a pair of really large garden gloves. "Just get dressed and take what you can out of the hallway out onto the front lawn. Be careful not to hurt yourself. I'm going back on the roof to nail down the tarp. I want to be done before noon when the sun will be unbearable."

"What time is it now?" I didn't own a watch, but it looked pretty bright out to me already.

"It's nine-thirty," he said. "We've got some time, but I want to get everything closed so I can start-up the generator tonight."

"You've got a generator?"

"Yes."

"Oh, that's great," I said.

"Not really. If we run out of gas, we're still fucked," he said. "It could be weeks before the roads are clear to drive, and the gas supply will be low. I only intend to use it for a few hours a day."

"Still, it means I can cook us dinner, right? And boil more water if we need it?"

"I have to check that the circuit in the kitchen is isolated from the rest of this mess before I start the generator. I've got a grill, though, so we won't starve. Don't open the fridge. I should have mentioned it last night, but we need things to keep as long as possible. We don't want the bit of cold left in there escaping." He turned to get a spray bottle from the large square coffee table in the den where we'd had all the supplies before we moved to the fortress. "You'll need this." He sprayed my body with something that smelled funny, like licorice and nail polish.

"What is that?"

"It's mosquito spray. They're going to be everywhere soon."

"It stinks," I complained.

"Believe me, you'll thank me for it."

"Okay."

"Now, get dressed, and I'll see you before noon."

"Yes, sir."

I hoped for another kiss, but nope. Juan just turned and stormed away, climbing up to the roof through the gap in the ceiling. He was strong as Superman, and way sexier to me.

I shook my head, clearing it of wanton thoughts, and focused on what I needed to do.

The mess was overwhelming, to be honest. Just trying to take something out caused something else to fall. Some of the wet wall panels crumbled in my hands when I picked them up, making a bigger mess on the way out. But I persisted, one bit at a time. I made two different piles of debris outside. One for just general junk and another for things that might be worth saving with a little care, or which might be useful in rebuilding. Outside was almost as much of a mess as inside. There were palm fronds everywhere. I had to move a few of those first, just to make room for my piles. There were large trees completely uprooted and tossed in the middle of the road, which would have to be cut down before we could leave the house. The destruction seemed to spread everywhere. Nothing was where it should be. There weren't any neighbors around for quite a distance, but I found a mailbox with the name Kensington and the house number sixty-three painted on it. Whoever the Kensingtons were, I hoped they'd fared better than their cute little birdhouse mailbox. Hank had shredded the wilderness, which had surrounded the house, to bits. This might take forever to put right again. I imagined the county would send help, eventually. But for now, it was just us.

I was halfway down the hall on the cleanup when I lifted a piece of roof tile and saw the corner of what looked like a family album. I cleared around it and opened it up. There were pictures in there of Juan and his family, when he was a little boy, in the house that had been just like this one before Andrew swallowed it up.

I recognized his father right away. Juan was just like him, tall, large and muscular, but his father had short, cropped hair. He was a military man too—there were a few pictures of him in uniform, looking all serious and handsome. His mother was a beautiful woman, taller than me, based on how she looked standing next to her husband. She also had long dark hair, and an hourglass figure with a generous bosom. They all looked like they belonged together and life was beautiful.

Juan was just an adorable kid. In one photo, he smiled from ear to ear, with a missing front tooth, and held up a Christmas present. I could see him shaking it to figure out what was inside. I wanted to give that little kid a hug. He looked around six and wouldn't have been much older than that when the house he sat in vanished. I tried to do the math in my head. If Juan was thirty-seven, then he would have been around seven when Andrew destroyed his life.

That's old enough to understand death, but seeing his father killed and his mother injured would have been devastating. How did he manage it?

The photo album was not in bad condition, considering what it had gone through. It had to have survived Andrew, too. I took it into the kitchen and patted it dry with a dish-cloth, wiping the water droplets from each plastic covered page, then left it on the table in the den and got back to work.

By the time Juan finished covering the roof securely with a blue tarp, I had put the hallway to rights again—as good as it would get without outside help. I had checked the spare rooms along the way and they were a wreck. So was the master bedroom. The bed was unusable. The mattress had soaked up rain like a sponge and would need to be tossed out. Strangely, the walk-in closet had survived the storm, unscathed, as had the master bathroom.

The damage was so random that I couldn't really wrap my mind around it. It had to have been a tornado, licking at us from the side. That was the thing about hurricanes. They brought plenty of company along to spread the wreckage.

It was getting hotter as the morning wrapped-up and I was tired and sweaty. I grabbed a bottle of water from our supply bags under the dining room table and sat on the new front porch slab to rest. That's where Juan found me when he climbed down from the roof.

"You did a good job, Jenny," he said, joining me on the slab. "Much more work than I expected."

"I'm really not useless, you know," I said.

"I never thought you were," he said, taking the bottle of water I passed to him. "Reckless, maybe. A little crazy, for sure. But not useless."

"This is not that different from life after Dad," I said, being much more candid than I probably should have been.

"Handle one thing at a time and you can pretend everything is normal."

"What happened to your father?"

"He's in an asylum," I said. "He's been in and out of one for most of my life."

"Oh, I'm sorry about the crazy remark. I was just poking fun at your wild nature, but that was insensitive."

"You didn't know," I said, shrugging it off. "Besides, I'll be the first to say it—we Banks are a little more nuts than average."

That was probably the wrong thing for me to say, too. There's nothing funny about mental illness. I knew that better than most. I deflected, though, making light of my family's dark side, just out of spite. It wasn't just Dad's schizophrenia, or even Mom's debilitating dark moods, or her habit of self-medicating with alcohol, which I'd inherited. Sometimes I scared myself, to be honest. But going through all that only made me feel more confident that life was a fleeting thing, and you had to take your joy wherever you found it.

Hank had proven that to be true.

Juan and I sat in silence for a while, letting the hurricane-cleared air cleanse the heaviness I'd introduced into the conversation. "Come inside and I'll make you lunch," he said, putting his hand on my knee.

"I can cook."

"We'll cook tonight, after I check the outlets for safety and maybe start the generator. Or I'll grill something up. For now, I've got tuna surprise."

"What's the surprise?"

"No mayo. I don't want to open a jar because it spoils too quickly."

"So, it's just canned tuna on bread?"

"Packed in oil, and mixed with fancy French mustard."

"Sounds delicious."

I was starving at this point and would have gladly eaten the canned Vienna sausages I'd noticed in the pantry the night before, when I went looking for pain killers and found the beer. Though maybe Juan was saving those for dinner.

"How long have you been prepping for this?" I followed him inside.

"Since the last one."

"Well, I'd say we came out pretty good, thanks to you."

"No, Jenny," he said. "The hurricane has passed, but the trouble has only started."

Chapter 6

So we started the cleanup, made a mess, and came to an understanding.

WE TOOK our sandwiches and more water into the den to eat, and Juan immediately noticed the photo album on the table.

"Where'd you get this?"

"It was in the hallway," I said. "I cleaned it up, but it's in pretty good condition. There are a few things outside you may want to look through which could be saved. Some linens I could wash by hand and hang-up to dry…"

"I thought I'd lost it." He caressed the cover with his large hand. "I thought it had blown away."

"Nope, it was just hiding under a bit of rubble."

Juan put the album back on the table and pulled me into his arms, squeezing me so tight I felt like I'd fallen into the grasp of a sea monster. He was slippery with sweat, but it felt fantastic there. Juan gave me a tender kiss which seemed to go on forever, and I wish it had.

"Thank you, Jenny Banks." Juan ruined it for me. I thought we were past this.

"Please, just call me Jenny," I insisted. "I like it when you *just* call me Jenny."

"Thank you, Jenny," he said, caressing my cheek.

"Can I be *your* Jenny now?"

"No, I don't think that's a good idea," he said. "I got carried away last night, but you're too young for me, Jenny. You need someone who is interested in the things you're interested in, someone you can relate to. You don't want an old man bossing you around."

"But I do," I said. "I definitely want that. I mean, not that you're an old man—you're not. You're still young and, honestly, hot as hell. But I want what we had last night. And what we were about to have before Hank so rudely inter-rupted us. I want someone who will bring some structure to my life, who will keep me in line and protect me, and punish me and cuddle me. Someone I can respect and call my Sir. I have met no one I wanted like that until I met you."

"Jenny," he said. "It's all this excitement of the storm you're feeling. It's not real. Right now, you're stranded and you're feeling lost. Like, this isn't real life. When real life returns, you're going to feel differently."

"No, I won't," I argued. "Honest, Juan. This is… I mean, it's an awful situation and I'm sorry we had to go through it, but what I feel is real and it's intense. I want to see where it goes."

"Jenny, I want a woman who I can dominate completely. Do you understand? It's not something I can expect from someone like you."

"Why? Because I'm Anglo? I mean, were you looking for someone Hispanic, is that it?"

"No, it has nothing to do with that. I've met plenty of Hispanic women it wouldn't work out with either. But I don't feel I can ask that of you. I can't believe it's something you would want, even if you tell me it is."

"Is it because of my family history?"

"No," he said. "Honestly, Jenny, it's what I said. You are very young and I'm not sure you want what I want. Right now, you think you do because the hurricane brought us together. It's almost like a near-death experience thing, where you feel things more intensely. But you don't really know me at all and you can't know what it will be like to be my sub."

"And you don't know me, so you can't know that it wouldn't be exactly what I want—what I've wanted for a long time, but couldn't find," I said. "Except you know how my body feels about it."

"What happened last night was wrong. The roof saved us from making a bigger mistake. Let's just get through this part of it, then you'll go back to your life and I'll go back to mine."

I rose from the couch and stormed off, having lost my appetite. I headed to the front yard and wandered around a bit, looking at the destruction. Men didn't turn me down. Not that I chased men often. In fact, I rarely had to, but if I said 'yes' just once, they were totally onboard. Juan was wrong about my being too young. I was sure of it, and I hated being stuck here with him now in the middle of all this chaos with an extra layer of awkward added to an already unpleasant situation.

I didn't really know what to do with Juan, but fine. We could be survival mates if that's what he wanted. I could deal. After all, he wasn't *that* special. I resented the heck out of him, though, because he'd made me feel safe enough to open up about this side of myself and he'd given me a taste of something that was just so very much what I had longed for… *Fine. Survival buddies it is.*

"You can't throw a tantrum every time you don't get your way." Juan's deep voice startled me out of my tight skin.

"I'm not throwing a tantrum, just getting some fresh air."

"Go back inside and eat your lunch," he commanded. "You worked really hard and you need to keep up your energy and drink plenty of water. We still have a lot to get done before tonight."

"Like what?"

"Protecting the front of the house is the priority now. I'm going to need your help for that."

"Okay, fine."

Juan came up to me, too close for comfort, and caressed my cheek again with his huge hand. "Don't pout."

"It's none of your business if I do."

"Don't be a brat."

"What do you care?"

"Go eat your lunch, Jenny Banks."

I stuck my tongue out at him and earned a swat on the ass. So I guess I won that round.

Then I went inside and ate his *just awful* tuna sandwich.

The man needed help.

It took a lot of work to board up the front again, mainly because so much of it had blown away. Fortunately, Juan had stored a good amount of large plywood panels in the garage, which had held up just fine. That became the new, far less welcoming, front entrance of the house. Everything else, we just covered in plywood. When our plywood wall was complete, Juan brought out a can of black spray paint, painted the house address and added a warning in large block letters: INTRUDERS SHOT ON SIGHT.

"Seriously? You're going to shoot anyone who wanders by?"

"Yes."

"Why?"

"Because soon the looting will begin and I want everyone to understand I will not take it."

"Do you have a gun in the house?"

"I'm a trained sniper, Jenny Banks. I'm armed for war if that's what it takes."

"It won't be so bad, will it?"

"Let's hope not," Juan said. "Now I'm going to handle the loose electrical wires. There are a lot of those to fix. Why don't you take a break and relax for a while? Maybe read a book or something. I have a few in the den. You did plenty of hard work today and you need a little time off."

I smiled at him. "You just want me out of your hair while you work."

"Yes, that's correct."

"Do you think you'll be able to start the generator so I can cook us some decent food? I think I should be in charge of meals from now on because it's not your top skill."

"I saw too many loose wires and I don't want to risk turning anything on until I know we won't spark a fire. For now, we're good, even if the city brings the power back on. I turned off the mains. I can grill something, though."

"At least let me marinate whatever you're going to grill, or do something to it besides add mustard."

"The sandwich wasn't that bad. It's fuel, which is all you need."

"Most of what you just said is wrong, but whatever." I stepped through the side door of the garage to wash up a bit and relax, as he suggested. Honestly, I needed a long cold shower and a change of clothes, but neither of those was available. The hall bathroom was still mostly usable, despite the damage, now that Juan had covered up the roof with tarp and I'd cleared out what remained of the debris. The water we'd stored in the sink and tub had partially blown away, but the storm's rains refilled it, which was helpful. That rain water might not be safe enough to drink, but it worked just fine for washing. I wet a washcloth in it and wiped my face and body, taking a sort of standing bath, and then sprayed on some of Juan's Brut body spray. Then I snuck over to the master bedroom, walking naked, to search for another spare t-shirt I might borrow from Juan's collection and a fresh pair of boxers. I'd honestly had enough of the lining on his swim shorts chafing my skin.

When I checked the damage in his room earlier, I hadn't really gone into Juan's closet. Now I poked around.

I found some interesting items in a large storage box on a shelf which suggested Juan was seriously into BDSM or a kidnapper. There were several lengths of soft silk rope, neatly tied in bundles, and handcuffs, and a ball gag with holes in it, a blindfold, a few intriguing instruments of pain I'd never seen before, some chains, a gigantic metal butt plug, and a couple of curiously shaped alien dildos.

"The paddle is hanging behind the door, if you need that," Juan said, startling me. He sounded angry again, which really worked for him. "When did I give you permission to go through my things?"

"I needed to change," I said, turning around, though I couldn't really face him. I just stared at my toes. "The clothes you gave me this morning got gross with sweat and stuff. I can wash them in the tub and put them up to dry, but I need something else to wear for now. I can't really go around naked. It's not safe with all the splinters around. Plus, you said there would be mosquitos and I don't want to be covered in repellent…"

I was talking a lot, but mainly it was to cover for his

silence. I looked up. He stood there at the door of the closet next to the very large and mean looking paddle I hadn't noticed earlier, his arms crossed, his muscles flexed, looking like he really disapproved of me. But there was something else in his eyes, too. Hunger. He couldn't hide that. I will say, I look pretty good naked, or so I've been told by people who could judge it objectively. I stood up straight, pushing my chest out and gave him an innocent smile.

"This will not work, little one," he said, slowly, with a deep menace in his tone.

That made me shiver, and I lost my confidence for a split second. Maybe I *was* biting off more than I could chew with this man. But I wanted to bite him so badly, especially his bulging pecs.

He stepped closer. I thought he might grab me and do something deliciously wicked, but he reached for one of several shirts which were still neatly folded on a shelf right in front of me, tossed one on my head and then grabbed a pair of boxer shorts and threw that on top.

"Get dressed and get out. Do not come in here again without permission."

"Yes, sir." I grabbed the two items of clothing, slipping first into the red plaid boxer shorts, then into the khaki green t-shirt. He just stood there, watching me dress. I couldn't get out because he took up all the room on the way to the door.

"Um, I need to..." I started, but I didn't get to finish. Suddenly, he pressed me up against the far wall of the closet with one hand on my neck. His other hand roved under my shirt to find my right breast and give my nipple an excruciatingly hard squeeze. I squealed in pain. Some of the ache came from my pussy, which had just woken up to the possibility that she might finally see some action and had suddenly cheered up.

"Is this what you want, little one? Do you want to be my

rag doll? Do you want to be used until you weep for mercy?" His hand moved away from my breast to slip down under the elastic of the shorts. Juan reached right between my legs and grabbed my pussy like he owned it, which I really wished he would. "Do you want to serve a Master who will take you and take you until you can't even bear to think of any other man on the planet but him? A man who will keep you on your knees, servicing his cock in every way imaginable? A cruel Dom who will punish his sub for every infraction, no matter how slight, who will set up strict rules for her body and her life, who will take her any way he pleases any time he wants? Is that what you're asking for, my little... wayward... slut?"

I just stared at him for a moment because I wanted to collect my thoughts and remember how speech worked. First, I had to remember how to breathe again. When I did, it was just a jagged, raspy breath. His dark eyes held mine captive, and his fingers tightened around my throat.

"Yes," I said, finally. "Please."

"I must be out of my mind," he said, shaking his head. He released my neck and stepped out of the closet. "Get the fuck out, Jenny Banks. Don't come in here again."

"No," I said.

Juan turned again, blocking my exit, a fierce expression on his face.

"I don't have time for this, Jenny. You don't know what you want and I can't give you what you need. It's a matter of survival for us over the next few days—maybe weeks. You have a lot of bad habits to break and you can't even follow basic orders. So, no, Jenny, you can't be my sub. Now, stop messing around and get out of here. Go rest, like I said, and..."

"Please." I took a step forward and closed the gap between us, rubbing up against his hard body like a cat, looping my arms over his shoulders. "Give me a chance. You won't regret it."

"Jesus, Jenny." He pushed me away, but I moved forward, so he pushed me away again, gripping me by the shoulders so I couldn't budge. "I'll make you a deal."

"Okay." I looked at him, hoping he would admit he felt the same crackling static between us I felt, and give in to it, setting off a bomb which would engulf us in flames. "If you can behave from now until this evening, and do everything I say, I will scratch your itch tonight," he said, wrapping his arm around my back to pull me against his tense muscles. He was on fire, and sweaty, and yet he felt and smelled wonderful, salty and earthy and raw—just delicious. "I can't promise anything more. I don't think you really want what I need, and I don't think it would work between us. But I'll get you over this… whatever it is you're going through."

"I won't get over it."

"Jenny, I can only promise to get you over this need. That's it. No commitment. No relationship."

"I can live with that," I said, and at the time I really believed I could. I needed him so badly that any crumb would do.

"You have to earn it."

"Yes, sir." I smiled sweetly at him. Juan pulled me into a fierce kiss. His stubble scratched and his tongue demanded, and his hand moved down to squeeze my ass. He dug his thick fingers into my flesh, reviving the dull ache deep in my muscles from the spanking he'd given me with the wooden spoon the night before. "I'll be good," I said when he finally let me go.

"Starting now."

"Yes."

"Go take a nap. You need to rest and I've got stuff to do. I'll wake you up when it's time for dinner."

"Let me help you with that, please. It's nothing personal, but your cooking skills are lacking."

"Are you going to be a smart-ass right off the bat?" His grin told me he wasn't angry with me, more amused than anything else.

"No, sir," I said. "Just trying to be helpful."

He smacked my ass as I left the closet and headed to the den, determined to be a good girl.

For a few hours, anyway.

Chapter 7

The grill and no chill on our first night of the Hank-pocalypse

IT WAS TOO hot to sleep, and I honestly didn't think I was tired enough to nap, but I still passed out. I guess it was all that hard work.

I dreamt of the storm—that train going forever—swallowing up the world. Juan and I were the last two humans left, determined to repopulate the planet. I was so very horny. Maybe he was right. In another set of circumstances, I might never have wanted him. But when he woke me, with a gentle nudge on the shoulder instead of a splash of water on my face, I only wanted him more. He had cleaned up and changed, and he looked and smelled just scrumptious.

"Come, little one," he said. "Let's make dinner together."

"Did you turn on the generator?"

"Yes," he said. "Only for the kitchen, though. That way, we can keep things cold and we will use less fuel. We'll need the hurricane lamps in the rest of the house. There are too many damaged wires to risk turning on the power everywhere. It's okay to use the master bathroom to clean up. You should only use the hall bath to wash clothes."

"Okay, so what needs to be cooked first, so it doesn't spoil? Whatever you have, I'll come up with a good recipe for it."

Juan smiled. "I had put the meats in the deep freezer in the garage. They didn't get to thaw out before I turned on the generator. We can have whatever you want. I can turn on the grill and make some burgers, if you'd like that. It will be cooler outside anyway, and I cleared up the patio so we can sit out there comfortably."

"That sounds good. Do you have any vegetables in the fridge? I can make a salad."

"Yeah, there are a few things in there you can use. But bring them out. You can mix the salad on the patio while I grill. It's too hot in the kitchen."

It was a beautiful evening, if you could look past all the destruction. We still had some daylight to enjoy our meal, but the intense heat of mid-day and the early afternoon was behind us. I took advantage of some frozen pink lemonade which had softened in the refrigerator's freezer and some of the water I'd boiled the day before to make us something cold to drink. Juan had the radio going outside, keeping us updated on the news.

It was bad. The destruction was extensive, affecting Monroe and Dade County and parts of Broward. They estimated losses in the billions. The major highways were closed and there were power outages everywhere, which they said might last for weeks in some areas. It was a really early storm too, coming as it did in late July, so we still had until November to worry about a second storm or a third hitting us before they could fix everything.

"It's just like Andrew." Juan shook his head, as we sat

enjoying a cool breeze and his burgers, which were much better than Juan's tuna sandwiches. "Actually, this was a worse storm, but at least the house fared better this time."

I couldn't wrap my head around how one storm could bring the entire world down around your ears and set you back decades in just a matter of hours. We had some modern conveniences, but only because Juan had prepared so well and only because we got lucky.

"So what happens now? I don't even have my phone to call anyone. Could I borrow yours?"

"Yes, you can try," he said. "I couldn't reach my contacts at the zoo. Their phones aren't working. I'd like to get there with the truck, just to check on the people who were on site and take them some supplies."

"Seriously? How could you even drive in this?"

"Carefully."

I took another bite of my burger and wished I could ask Juan for a beer to go with it. Though that would cancel my good girl status, and I was still very much looking forward to hooking up with Juan.

"Guess they canceled school, for now." I sighed.

"They canceled everything for now."

I stared at Juan's backyard pool, which was mostly empty, except for sticks and leaves. I felt like one of those leaves floating on what remained of the water in what used to be the deep end.

"Those guys who threw the party, are they related to you?"

"They're my cousins."

"And how did they get into the house?"

"The little assholes knew where I kept my spare key. They also knew I'd gone down to Key Largo for some fishing over the weekend. They didn't track the storm, though, so they weren't expecting me to come home early."

"Do you think they're okay?"

"Yeah, they'll be fine. Their dad has tons of money, so he probably flew them all out to New York to wait out the storm."

"How would they make a flight in time, though? I mean, when I woke up, the storm was practically here."

"Well, first, you were passed out for hours. I broke up the party at two in the morning and put those assholes in a taxi to take them home. They were in no condition to drive. Besides, their dad has his own jet, so he could have taken off before they closed the airport."

"Where's their car? Was it blown away too?"

"Probably. Assuming they drove here. Maybe they came over with someone."

"When I followed them from the club, they were in a fancy red sports car. Can't remember the type. It's all blurry, to be honest."

"How is that your life?" Juan sounded deeply disgusted with me, and I felt ashamed, which was not something I enjoyed feeling.

"So judgmental," I mumbled, speaking mostly to my burger, though Juan heard me.

He put down his burger and gave me a hard look. "Am I wrong?" His voice was a low growl, which made me all goose pimply, despite the warm evening. I should have just let it pass, or told him he was right, but Juan didn't know me well enough to pass judgment.

"Yes. You are very wrong. I am not just a party girl, you know. I raised myself and got myself to college. I'm not an idiot. I know I've done some dangerous things, but I need that danger—the excitement, the thrill—it's how I know I'm alive. Besides, life is short and youth is brief. I'm going to enjoy every minute of mine."

Juan just looked at me for a while. I couldn't tell what he

was thinking. His face was an inscrutable stone. When he finally spoke, there was a twisted grin on his lips. "You're so independent and feisty, but you want to be dominated?"

"Because it excites me, sexually. I can't explain why. The truth is, I drink and I party because I need to feel light, but it never really makes me light for very long. I still feel heavy the next morning. I don't want to feel heavy anymore. I've been in charge of myself for so long, and it's draining. I need someone I can trust to carry the weight for a while, or at least to share the load. Does that make sense?"

Juan went back to eating his burger again without answering. I think he was just digesting my words. I went back to eating too, swallowing my bitterness with every bite. After a while, he asked, "What makes you think you can trust me, Jenny Banks? You don't know me at all."

I scoffed at that. "You're not that hard to figure out, Juan Ruiz. I mean, you are hardworking and tough, but you can also be tender. You could have tossed me out on the street when the storm was coming, but you gave me shelter. You're well prepared for the unexpected, which shows some thoughtfulness and self-discipline, as well as resourcefulness. You are a solid, reliable man. While you spanked me real hard, I liked it. You have some terrible qualities too—like this insecurity you have about your age, for example—but on the whole you're on the positive side of the equation. You're way ahead of most men I've met in my life. And I'm incredibly attracted to you, which helps."

Again, Juan became a stone, and this time, his silence was longer. I expected him to tell me our deal was off and that I'd failed whatever test he had planned for me.

Instead, he pushed his chair back and smiled at me. "Come here," he said, patting his lap. I was done with my burger, anyway, and excited about getting started with the fun part of the evening. I sprang up and hopped around the table to perch myself on Juan's hard thigh. When I tried to drape my arms around his neck, he grabbed both my wrists and held them down on my lap.

"What did you mean when you said you want to feel light?"

"I just mean the thrill I get from a little danger and a little pain. It's like a high, better than drugs or alcohol. It helps lessen the load of just living my life. Do you know what I mean?"

He looked at me with a grin and tucked back a damp curl of my hair, which had fallen over my eyes, then he caressed the dimple on my chin with his thick index finger. "Is your life really so heavy? All you do is study and party, right?"

"No, that's not all I do." I scowled at him. "I have to manage my father's estate, you know. My mother is on a spa vacation or in rehab, depending on the day. Her head was never into protecting our assets. If I hadn't got smart about life on my own, our former financial advisors would have probably left us on the street. To be honest, I'm worried that something like that might happen if too much time passes without me checking in to say I'm alive."

"Poor little rich girl." He stroked my cheek.

"Don't do that. Stop making assumptions about me."

"You're not rich?"

"That's not the point. My father has spent more of his life in an asylum than at home, and my mother wouldn't give a shit if I was gone, except she'd be out of money real quick. The only people who actually care whether I'm alive or dead would probably be happier if I was dead."

"So why do you do such irresponsible things—things that could get you hurt or killed?"

"Because I've been alone with all that since I was six.

Sometimes I just need to forget all of it for a while. Other times, I don't care whether I survive the night."

"You don't mean that." He released my wrists to hold me closer, wrapping his arms around me.

"I do!" I was practically crying at this point. It was too horribly true, even if I had never admitted it to anyone before.

"Well stop," Juan commanded. "You're not allowed to hurt yourself."

"Who is going to stop me?" I asked, feeling hopeful about his answer.

"As long as you're with me, you will not talk like that, or think like that, or behave in any way that puts you in danger. I will not allow it."

"Does that mean what I think it means?"

"I don't know what it means, but for now, you're my responsibility," Juan said. "That has to be enough, at least until we figure out the rest."

"All right." I smiled at him, and his scowl softened a bit.

"I can give you my phone and you can call your financial advisors to tell them you're okay. Call your mother too. She may surprise you."

"I doubt it."

"Do it." He let go of me to reach into his pocket and grab his mobile phone, passing it to me.

"Yes, Sir."

So, perched like a pet on my would-be master's lap, I called the people who needed to hear from me, even if they didn't want to. The attorney who oversaw my father's trust seemed somewhat relieved to hear I hadn't been blown away like Dorothy. I hadn't expected that, but I guess he didn't want to be saddled with handling my mother on his own. She did not know there had been a hurricane in South Florida. She asked me not to bother her with trifles if I was just fine. Mom sounded drunk, slurring her words, which was no surprise. After all, it was a day of the week.

"I may not get home for a while though, Mother," I said. "The destruction here is pretty severe. I don't know when airports will open again."

"Were you planning to come home?"

I rolled my eyes, though only Juan could see it. "Yes, Mother, I had planned to fly home for Father's birthday at the end of the month. Remember? We were going to visit him. You should go, anyway, if I can't make it."

"I don't like that place. I don't think I can handle it on my own."

"Too bad, Mother. You'll have to go. He needs to see family."

"He doesn't even recognize me half the time."

"That's not true. Dad recognizes you very well. You just don't like what he sees."

There was silence on the line for a moment while my mother processed that. She knew what I meant. My father would sometimes weep over how much he loved her and, at other times, accuse her of ruining his life. Both were sadly true.

"You're a horrible daughter," she complained. "I raised a monster."

"You raised nothing. I became a monster on my own."

Then I hung up because I didn't want to say more to my mother in front of Juan. I'd already said too much.

"You sound different when you talk to those people," Juan observed as he took his phone back. "Thirty years older, and much too formal."

"I told you, I'm not as young as you think," I said. "I haven't been for too long. Anyway, I'm sorry about all of that. Thanks for letting me use your phone. I'll pay you for the long distance charges."

"Don't make me angry. I don't want to spank you right this minute."

"You don't?" I smiled at him, flashing lashes. "What do you want to do with me?"

"Maybe lighten your load a bit." He kissed my lips gently and left me wanting more. "We have to clear all this up and organize inside first. Night is coming and we have to be ready for it. Can you handle that?"

That worried me. I knew he'd mentioned looters, but it seemed too soon for that. "Do you expect trouble?"

"Always."

Chapter 8

I almost got what I wanted and, as usual, that was a problem.

WE TIDIED up after our meal and arranged the mattresses Juan had first tied up around the table to form his protective fortress into a neat double bed at the back of the den, next to the sliding glass doors with the screens so we could get some fresh air while we slept. Juan went into the small office by the den, behind the kitchen, where he'd first found me sleeping. He came back with a sniper rifle, which he set up behind the couch by his side of the bed, as well as two handguns.

Juan asked me whether I could shoot, but he was skeptical when I said I could. He took me out to the backyard to prove it. I delighted in the blend of shock and admiration on his face when I knocked over each of the bottles he'd set up for me to practice on.

"Are you going to prove to me *you* can shoot now?" I asked, teasing.

He grinned. "No, you'll have to take the Army's word for

it." The smile was forced, though. There was something in his eyes which looked like regret to me.

"Were you out there long?"

"I'm still there."

"I'm sorry." I reached out to stroke his arm, hoping it would comfort him, but he flinched as if the affection burned his skin.

"Don't be. I'd rather be a killer than a fool."

Juan recovered quickly from that dark revelation and kissed the tip of my nose. It was weird, almost like he had dropped his experience of war into a black hole of memory and was ready to play the part of a well-balanced human being. But I wasn't buying it. I knew too much about broken people, being one myself.

"So, what kind of trouble do you expect?"

"It might be nothing tonight. But it could be anything soon. We're far enough away from most people that it will take a while for anyone to reach us, but people get desperate. Desperate people do irrational things. Then there are the natural born assholes who see every tragedy as an opportunity to enrich themselves. Most of those work in offices, but some freelance on the streets. There will be thieves roaming around soon enough, looking for vulnerabilities. When they come here, they come to die."

"Not if, but when?"

"Unfortunately, yes. There's no doubt they'll come. It's only a matter of time. But don't worry about that. You can shoot any asshole that steps on our lawn, and I'll back you up."

"Fun." I smiled at him and rose on tip-toe to plant a kiss on his chin. He grabbed me on the way there and pulled me into a passionate kiss instead. His breath was hot and his mouth was lush, full lips and a thick, strong, raspy tongue. He knew what to do with it, teasing my own, making my palate tingle and my hunger grow. With one large hand, he held my head so I couldn't break away—not that I intended to. I could have kissed Juan for hours. His other hand gripped my butt like he wanted to break it, and I sure wished he would. He lifted me up to press me against his hard length. I was back to feeling hopelessly horny. Maybe a little less hopeless, since I knew he felt the same. But Juan had already shown me he could change his mind about wanting me quickly.

I had to fix that about him.

"So what now?" I asked, breathless, when he finally let me go.

"Now we scratch that itch of yours, beautiful," he said. "And if you're still able to walk in the morning, we'll see what comes next."

Then Juan hoisted me to his waist. I wrapped my arms around his neck and knotted my legs around his torso, grinning as he carried me to the sofa, where he sat down with me straddling him.

"Take your top off, baby," he commanded, his hands firmly planted on my broad, round ass. We had a good palm to butt ratio, which I thought boded well. "Give me a good look at those bountiful tits of yours."

I pulled off the t-shirt in a rush, which left my frizzy, curly hair running wild in all directions, but I didn't care. Juan didn't seem to mind either. All his attention went to my breasts, which he squeezed and kneaded, then slapped. I sighed. Then he pinched my nipples so hard that I squeaked. "That's nothing, baby. Clamps are worse, and you'd be wearing those, eventually. Are you sure this is what you want?"

"Yes, please, don't stop."

He poked his fingers through the gap in the boxers he'd loaned me to reach between the cleft of my lower lips and squeezed my clit just as tightly as he had pinched my nipples. "Oh, God, Juan," I cried out, as every sensitive nerve in my vulva came to life and my core ignited.

"Up," he ordered, smacking my butt. I hated to leave the comfort of his lap, to lose the delicious contact between my inner thigh and his warm erection, but I rose, just as he ordered, standing between his knees. He pulled down my shorts and turned me around. "Bend over, put your hands on the coffee table, and spread your legs apart."

I felt like I was going through the weirdest gynecological exam of my life as Juan appraised my vulva, tracing the folds with his fingertips, pinching and pulling my labia, and finally penetrating me with two thick fingers. I pushed back against his hand and he slapped my ass, a sharp sting rushing through me. "Stay still," he commanded. I whimpered when he pulled his fingers out, regretting the loss. Juan parted my back cheeks and circled the tight pucker of my ass. "How would you feel if I fucked you here?"

"I'd like it," I admitted.

A sharper smack on my butt broke the silence like a popped balloon and caused me to rise on the heels of my feet despite his command to be still. "Don't lie to me."

"It's true. I think if you fucked me in the ass, it would feel fantastic."

"Why?"

"I just imagine it would. Anything you do to me would feel great."

"You're not supposed to like it. When I fuck you in the ass, it's for punishment. If you were mine, I would fuck you rough when you needed a lesson."

"I mean, it would definitely send a message that I was bad. I just… You can do whatever you want to me. I'm going to enjoy it."

"Then your punishment will be denial. No orgasms for

bad girls. No treats. No playing with yourself to satisfy what I refuse you, either. You will stay on the edge until I'm sure you've learned a lesson."

"But I've learned my lesson," I said. "I haven't asked you for another beer, have I? Lord knows I could use a drink."

Smack. The spank was so hard that my hands slipped forward on the table, and tears filled my eyes. "No more alcohol for you." A second smack followed on the other cheek, just as strong. "You stay sober."

"Yes, sir," I said, sniffling, as I turned my head to look up at him, where he stood looking all hot and shiny. Juan had removed his shirt and his chest glistened with tiny pearls of perspiration. I wanted to lick it all off. Still, I kept my place, bent over and wiggled my ass at him. "Are you *not* going to fuck me now?"

"I am definitely going to fuck you, baby," he said, stroking my pussy and circling my clit he'd set on fire earlier with a pinch. Then he dipped one finger in my entrance, swirling it around. "This tight, drenched little channel needs filling."

Juan pulled out a condom from his pocket.

"I'm on the pill, you know," I said. "You don't need to worry about me getting pregnant. I'm never having kids." I don't know why I added the last part, but it just came out. Maybe my mother was still on my mind. It gave Juan pause. Which was strange since it was none of his business.

"I'm going to use one," he said, recovering from wherever he'd gone in his thoughts.

"Whatever you prefer."

"Do you have a lot of unprotected sex while you're drunk?"

Now he was questioning his choices again, and I couldn't really blame him. Encouraging him to fuck me without protection was careless, but he made me feel defensive again.

"No, I don't have unprotected sex, sober or otherwise, and I rarely fuck when I'm drunk."

"How would you even know, honestly?"

"What?"

"You take such risks. What if someone put something in your drink? How would you stop them?"

"Look, if you're only going to lecture me, can I straighten up?"

"I'm not trying to lecture you, but damn it, Jenny. How have you survived?"

I stood up and turned to face him, without waiting for him to say I could. Sex was off. The wind had changed again. "I'm not usually as drunk as I was the other night, Juan. I think I was just exhausted, too, which is why I passed out. And if someone did something to me while I was unconscious, I'd know."

Juan caressed my cheek, but somehow it felt like a slap in the face. I was furious. I stepped away from him, gathered my scattered shirt and shorts, put them back on again, then rushed out into the backyard to get some fresh air.

Juan let me go, which felt terrible, even if I only would have bitten his head off for following me out there. He had no right to make me feel bad about myself. Besides, I felt like he was a cock tease. I mean, he was teasing me with the possibility of getting his cock. And I still wanted it, which was awful, and it made me wonder whether I respected myself enough.

I should have been worried about safe sex too, but I hadn't given it much thought with Juan. While the suddenness and intensity of desire I felt for him was more than anything I'd ever experienced before, maybe Juan was right. Maybe I only found him sexy because of Hank. It could be some sort of post-traumatic survival instinct which urges you to mate, or whatever. Maybe I had no business playing these games with him. Maybe I should have been the one demanding he use a condom.

I knew Juan could only judge my character by how I'd acted so far, and it wasn't a pretty picture. First, he'd found me passed out drunk, and then I was trying to get drunk again right before the storm hit. Then there was that raw moment between us in the kitchen, which I still couldn't get out of my mind. And all the other flirting back and forth. But he wanted me too! He couldn't deny that.

Maybe I'd made it too easy for him. Yes, I had been impetuous, but maybe I was right. We could be perfect together. The two of us, messed up as we were, could have something wonderful. Why couldn't he see that?

I didn't mean love, by the way. I didn't actually believe in love. It was such a loaded word. It was a bullet to the brain. I didn't love Juan, and I knew he didn't love me. He didn't even like me. Besides, we'd just met each other, for heaven's sake. I meant sex. Only sex.

I had a strong feeling that Juan and I could be desperately in lust with each other. We could enjoy some kinky companionship. What the hell was wrong with wanting that?

I sat out on the patio alone, stewing, soothed by the clean night breeze. The usual steam of the South Florida summer had cleared out. Hank must have sucked it all up. The mosquitos hadn't shown up yet either and the sky above was amazing. With no lights around, there was nothing but stars for miles. It was quiet enough, except for the croaking and odd crinkling on the ground, as the toads, racoons, birds and other creatures of South Florida did their own damage checks and reconstructed their habitat.

Their night song soon put me to sleep. I awoke again,

only briefly, to feel Juan collect me in his arms and carry me indoors to lie on the mattress he'd set up in the den. I pretended to still be asleep as he snuggled up against me, holding me against his chest, wrapped in his muscular arms like his teddy bear. Maybe he needed some comfort, too. I don't know. He was hard. I could feel his erection pressed on my butt, but I had no hope of enjoying it anymore. And I would not act like I wanted it. Too bad. He'd have to make the next move.

Eventually, I fell into a deeper sleep. This time I didn't dream of Hurricane Hank. I dreamt of being a different girl, who might have a happy life with someone—anyone. The sort of life Juan's mother seemed to have in the family album I'd cleaned up. But my dream was brief, and I woke up alone on the mattress the next morning, no better off than I was the day before. Worse. Juan was gone. He hadn't even left a note.

Chapter 9

In which I got lost and found two scary snakes, but I liked the second one better than the first.

I SEARCHED THE WHOLE HOUSE. I called up to the roof and then went for the stepladder in the garage and saw that Juan's truck was gone. He'd just left without telling me he was going, which seemed really rude and irresponsible. After all, what was I supposed to do by myself in all this chaos?

At first, I just tried cleaning up the rest of the house, but then I ran out of things to clean that didn't require major reconstruction. So I cleaned myself in the master bathroom. The running water was back, and clear, which I thought boded well, but I wasn't sure whether it was safe to drink so I brushed my teeth with a little bottled water instead, using a new toothbrush I found in Juan's toiletry cabinet. I borrowed another of Juan's awful tacky swim trunks—this one with huge hot pink starfish on a turquoise background—and one of his khaki army t-shirts, and put those darned beach shoes back on. I looked like some kind of surfer clown, but this was just about covering my body at this point. I wasn't trying to impress anyone. Not that I expected anyone to be around. I combed my hair out with my fingers to untangle my frizzy curls a bit and headed out of the garage.

I considered, for a moment, whether Juan would want me to stay put watching over the place instead, but if he had wanted that, then he should have said so. I was sick of being stuck, and I wanted to see how far I could get on foot. Maybe the city had sent someone to clear the main roads. Maybe I could call an Uber soon, and get the hell out of there, and never have to see Juan again. Though that was unlikely since I'd lost my phone.

Anyway, I didn't plan to be gone too long. I knew I probably wouldn't get far in my odd clothes and odder footwear, but I hadn't imagined I'd be up against an obstacle course of this magnitude. I should have expected it, given what I'd seen from the house, but the up-turning of the world went on for miles. The road became meaningless. I climbed over some trunks and walked around others. I followed the path of the storm in reverse, and converse. Soon I was as topsy-turvy as the world itself. I had no familiar markers to guide me back to Juan's house. I was lost amid this fallen jungle, thirsty and hot, and feeling foolish. I sat on a trunk for a while, holding my head in my hands, and wept in frustration. I should just have stayed put.

Then, to make things worse, I saw something slithering through the broken branches of the fallen oak I sat on and soon I recognized the distinctive black, red and yellow bands of a coral snake.

One of my roommates, Gillian, was studying to be a herpetologist. She had a book on snakes, which I'd found fascinating to leaf through on a rainy Saturday. I remember remarking that the coral snake was beautiful. Not so much in person, though. In person, it was terrifying. I shifted slowly on the trunk towards the exposed root of the tree, hoping not to bump into anything else dangerous as I put distance between myself and the disoriented venomous snake. As soon as I was far enough away that she might not leap out at me, I ran. Well, I rushed off. It was impossible to run very far without bumping into something else. I would have been grateful for a clearing where I could get a sense of direction, maybe even see the house. Then I heard the rattled buzzing of a chainsaw nearby, and I made my way through the wreckage toward that sound.

I know that walking *towards* a chainsaw sounds kinda crazy, but this wasn't Texas. I didn't expect a massacre. Besides, a working chainsaw meant there was another living human around—possibly several. Maybe the county had sent people to help clear the way? They probably had water. I really needed water, especially since my heart had been at my throat since I first saw the coral snake.

When I finally saw the chainsaw, the man wielding it was too familiar. Somehow, I'd run around this broken wilderness only to wind up face-to-face with the last person on Earth I wanted to see. Juan turned off the chainsaw and stared at me awhile, like I was a mirage or something.

"Why are you here?" he asked, finally putting down the saw, which made him only slightly less intimidating.

"I could ask you that," I said, putting my fists on my hips.

"It's obvious why I'm here." Juan lifted the chainsaw again. "But what the hell are you doing in the middle of all of this?" He swung the chainsaw around. "Dressed like that? Why couldn't you just stay at home? Like a normal person."

"Well, you just vanished! I got worried. Plus, I figured I'd check whether the county had sent anyone to fix up the roads."

"Nobody can get here," Juan said, putting down the saw

again and shaking his head. "Anything could have happened to you, Jenny Banks. The critters around here are spooked."

"I know. I saw a coral snake earlier."

"What? *Where?*"

"I don't know." I raised my palms at my sides. "Somewhere in the branches of a fallen oak. I got a bit turned around, so I'm not sure where I am anymore."

"You got *turned around?* So, what was your plan to get back?"

"Look, I'm hot and thirsty. Do you have any water?"

Juan shook his head again, but he headed for his big-wheeled jeep to drop the saw in the back and pull out a bottle of water from his cooler. He waved me over, irritated beyond words. Even angry and sweaty, he looked great, though. He probably looked better.

I needed not to be noticing or thinking about that. We were barely survival mates. He was a tease. I deserved better. I had sunstroke and chronic survival horniness. CSH. I'd just invented a new diagnosis. Maybe I could write a paper about it for my psych course: Hurricane Hank and the female libido. My professor would probably love it, horny bastard that he was.

I went over to Juan and thanked him for the bottle of water, but he only grunted and pointed at the passenger door as he went over to the driver's side. Once I was inside the truck, Juan started the engine and headed back toward home. He didn't say a word through the short bumpy ride back. I was grateful for the silence, honestly. I was still much too hot and tired to suffer through another lecture. He'd cleared enough of a path to get to the end of his street, but there was still a lot of cleanup to do. There was no way Juan could do it alone.

After we got back to the house, Juan's attitude changed. He slammed the door to the Jeep after parking in the garage, pulled his handgun out of its holster at his waist and signaled for me to wait in the garage while he went inside with his gun out, presumably checking for looters.

I thought he was being paranoid. Obviously, if we could barely get out of his block, then no one could get in. Still, I waited for him to come back to get me.

"When I tell you to stay put, you stay put," Juan said when he returned to the garage. "You don't go wandering around, leaving the house undefended, and trying to get yourself killed."

"But you didn't tell me to stay put. You said nothing. I woke up, and you were gone."

"I left you a note."

"No, you didn't."

Juan stormed out of the garage and went straight to the kitchen, expecting me to follow, which I reluctantly did. I felt a little foolish when he pointed at the note on the fridge held in place with a little Key West magnet in the shape of a pelican. The note read: *I'm going to clear out some stumps. Stay put. I'll be back in a few hours.*

"Well, I didn't see that. You should have woken me up to tell me you were going."

"You needed your rest, and I thought you had sense enough to check for a note. Even if you didn't see it, what made you think it was safe to go wandering around out there?"

I grabbed a bottle of water and drank half of it in a single long gulp. Then I took a deep breath. "Well, nothing happened."

"Because you got lucky," Juan said, coming uncomfortably close. He stroked my cheek. "You got lost and did not know how to get back. You almost got bit by a deadly snake." He rubbed his thumb along my damp lips. "You just love getting in trouble, don't you, baby?"

"No," I said, barely able to get the word out. I was transfixed again, lost in those dark eyes, framed by glistening thick dark lashes. Juan was sweaty, and it looked wonderful on him. Sweaty Juan was delectable. Angry Juan was devastatingly gorgeous. The man just looked good in any altered state. It made me want to get him riled up constantly, to be honest. "I would have figured out a way to get back here."

Juan ran his fingers through my damp hair, straightening it out a bit. I guess I must have looked awful at this point. Worse than I already looked to begin with, since I had no makeup on and I was sweaty too.

"I'm glad a snake did not bite you," he said, pulling me closer, his arm wrapped around my waist. "I would have hated it if you died out there."

"Really?"

"Really. I wouldn't know where to put your body at this point."

"Asshole." I laughed, slapping his chest.

Juan laced his fingers through mine, which had lingered resting against his damp t-shirt. "I'm not good at relationships. In fact, I'm awful at them," he whispered.

"That's okay," I said. "I don't want a relationship."

"It would just be sex."

"Yes."

"No commitment."

"None."

"I'm not saying I want to be responsible for you."

"Right."

His other hand slid down my back, cupping my butt, then squeezing hard.

"While you're here, you have to do everything I say, or there will be consequences."

"Yes, sir."

"Come, let's take a bath," he said.

"Where?"

"The master bathtub is pretty big."

I had eyed the bathtub with longing, earlier, while I was in the master bath. It was a jacuzzi, and very inviting even without the functioning jets. Still, I figured he'd be more practical than wasting all that water on a single indulgence.

"Don't you think we should save that for a special occasion?"

"This *is* a special occasion."

"Is it?"

"Oh, yeah, baby girl." He gave me a gentle kiss, more of an invitation than an invasion. "As special as it gets." I warmed up to the idea of forgiving him for being such a dick the night before.

"So you're not worried about me being a slut anymore?"

"No, I've decided you're going to be *my* little slut." He took the sting out of the insult with another gentle kiss.

"For as long as we're stuck together," I said, just to make the terms clear between us.

"Yes, after that, you can decide what you *really* want."

"Okay." I smiled, reaching around to grab his firm buttocks. "Actually, it will feel wonderful being neck deep in some cool water for a while."

"Yeah, you need it," he said. "You're all flushed from the sun. I want to cool you down before I heat you up again. Because, baby, you are going to burn."

"Stop talking, big boy," I purred. "Take me there."

He put his hand around my throat, stroking my pulse point gently with his thumb. "I'm not a boy, Jenny Banks. I haven't been since I was six."

Well, I thought, as I struggled not to melt into a puddle at his feet. That's something we have in common.

Juan poured some sort of bath oil, which smelled like eucalyptus and cedar, into the cold bath water. Though Juan didn't seem to go for any kind of special grooming products, he apparently allowed himself some luxuries. The pleasantly scented oil made the bath much more inviting.

He undressed me slowly and almost reverently—not that there was much to take off—but the gentleness with which he removed the swim trunks and t-shirt I'd borrowed from him made me feel shy. It was an unusual feeling. I didn't quite know what to do with it. I wrapped my arms around my breasts as he removed his own t-shirt. When he saw me, he put my arms at my sides. "No, little one. You don't hide from me now." I blinked at the gentle reprimand and followed the trail of his hands as he unbuttoned his fatigues. He'd gone full commando, so there was nothing between him and the rough military fabric. I wondered whether he was just leaving all his boxer shorts aside for me, but I didn't get to ask.

As soon as he lowered his fatigues, my eyes focused only on the overwhelming reality of his bizarre super-sized erection. I hadn't really got to see him properly at night before everything fell apart. Now, I had a full frontal view of his engorged cock, and it left me speechless. Juan had to be nearly eleven inches long and so wide that I couldn't imagine he would fit anywhere in my body. "It may hurt a little until you get used to it, but I won't break you. Your body is more flexible than you think." Obviously, my discomfort showed on my face.

"You should be a porn star," I said, still unable to take my eyes off the stiff boa constrictor protruding from his muscular lower abdomen.

He laughed. "Get in the tub, Jenny Banks."

"Please don't call me that."

"Okay, little one. Get in the tub, now, or I'll paint your bubble butt bright red."

"Yes, sir." I turned to step into the jacuzzi. The water was cool and clean and just felt wonderful against my overheated skin. Juan followed me in, though he took a seat on the opposite side and just stared at me for a while, which made me feel shy again.

"Jenny, I want you to dip yourself under the water completely now. Get that pretty hair of yours all wet."

I did as he asked, and when I came up again, I blinked away the droplets of water from my eyelashes and smiled at the man resting back against the tub with his arms up at his sides.

"Good girl," he said. "Now, I want you to take that sponge beside you, and the bar of soap, and bring them to me. Get up and walk them over."

When I stood up, the bathwater only came to just below my knees, so I was fully exposed to him. I took a couple of steps forward which brought me to stand between his spread hairy legs, and handed over the dry natural sponge and new bar of Dove soap. He took the sponge and soap bar and dipped them in the bathwater, then he passed the damp bar to me. "I want you to soap yourself up for me, baby. Get that beautiful little body full of suds."

"Standing up?"

"Yes, Jenny. I want to see you do it."

I started by rubbing the bar along my arms and my shoulders and neck, then over my chest. "Lift those big girls for me and be sure you get soap all around and under them."

I have larger breasts than most girls my size, and I've always been self-conscious about them. Soaping up my breasts as he watched was a little unnerving, but not as bad as what came next. When I reached my lower belly, Juan stretched out his hand to claim back the soap, and he asked me to put my foot on one of his hard thighs so he could wash my legs properly. That left me open to him, my mons near to the hard tip of his nose, and yet he took his time soaping up my foot, lathering my calf, and making sure the crease behind my knee was nice and soapy before he worked his way up my thigh, almost to my open pussy, but then he stopped. "Give me the other leg, please, Jenny."

I did as he asked. He tsked when he noticed a scratch on the side of that thigh, which I hadn't really been aware of up to that point. My body was so full of ache and need that the sting of a slight cut was barely perceptible to me. I hissed in a breath when he soaped up the cut. "Bad girl, getting yourself hurt for no good reason. We're going to address that when we're done with bath time, Jenny."

"How?"

"You wanted to get to know the bite of my paddle, right?"

"Not really."

"Of course you did," Juan said. "Why else would you be so very naughty, Jenny?"

"I um…"

"Shh, baby. Don't argue. Let's get you washed up first."

Juan picked up the damp sponge with had been floating near his chest, lathered it up with the soap, and brought the wet, sudsy sponge right up to the gap between my legs, soaping my folds gently and reaching right through to the crack of my ass. It was so intimate an intrusion, though gentle, that I gasped and my knees buckled a bit. "Hold on to my shoulders so you don't fall, baby."

I heeded his command, my hands resting on the bulging muscles between his neck and shoulders. He rinsed the sponge and brought it back full of water to clear away the soap until my pussy and my ass were clean. I thought he'd rinse off the rest of the soap on my body at some point, but he put down the sponge and began stroking my folds gently with his fingers, teasing my nub. I felt electrified. All my nerve endings lit up, and every cell in my body quivered.

"Jenny," he said, as he stroked, bringing me closer and closer to orgasm. "I'm going to spank you so hard with my paddle that you'll be weeping for mercy. There will be none. Then I'm going to make you suck my cock. After that, I'm going to fuck this tight little pussy, and then I'm going to fuck your ass. When I'm done with you today, you won't feel like walking very far again for a while. Do you understand?" He pinched my clit hard.

"Ow-ah." A gasp of pleasure cut off my complaint.

"Say, yes, sir." He spanked my pussy hard.

"Ow-ow!"

"Jenny?" He spanked my pussy a second time, even harder.

"Yes, sir."

"Beg me to punish you for being a bad girl, Jenny." Juan slipped one of his fingers into my entrance. It slid in easily. I was drenched with desire, especially after he'd smacked my pussy.

"Please, sir," I said, though I struggled to speak in anything but pants at this point. "Punish me for being a bad girl."

"Wash me first, Jenny."

I knelt in the water and washed all of Juan, lathering the sponge with soap and running the sudsy sponge over every delectable muscle. Then I slipped the sponge under the water to wash his ball sack and cock. I let go of the sponge and wrapped my fingers around the shaft, enjoying the feel of his hardness in my fist. With a wicked grin, he pulled my hand away after I stroked him a few times. "Lusty little slut. You're going to get all the cum you want out of me. Don't worry."

Finally, he sat me between his legs and washed my back,

rinsing off all the soap from my body. He left my breasts for last and took his time, pinching my stiff nipples until I whimpered. Finally, he kissed my right shoulder. "Baby girl, bath time is over. It's punishment time."

"Yes, sir," I said, eager to get started. I did not know what awaited me, really, but I meant what I had said the night before. Anything that Juan might do to me would feel delicious.

"Wrap a towel around yourself and go back to the den. Don't forget to put on your beach shoes. I don't want you walking through the bedroom and hallway barefoot."

"Yes, sir," I said, rising out of the tub to comply. He didn't move. "Are you coming?"

"I'll be right behind you."

Chapter 10

I got more punishment than I thought I could handle and loved every minute until the last.

I WAITED ANXIOUSLY in the den for Juan to arrive. Though he'd told me what he had planned, I couldn't really accept any of it as real. The sun shone through the sliding glass doors which led to the patio. We were practically outside in this room. If anyone came by the broken backyard, they would see. Of course, given the circumstances, we were unlikely to be interrupted. But this all just felt like something that should happen in the dark, not that I wanted to wait until nighttime. I didn't want to have to wait another minute.

Juan didn't seem to mind the sunlight in the least. When he came to the den, bare chested with a towel wrapped low around his waist, wielding the large paddle in one hand and a handful of condom packages in the other, he opened the sliding glass doors.

"It's too hot in this house. We'll want some fresh air. Come to the patio, please, Jenny."

"You don't expect me to go outside naked."

"I do."

"Why?"

"Because it's what I'm asking you to do."

"But…"

"There's no one around for miles. It's just you and me. It will be more comfortable out there where there's a breeze than in here."

"What about the mosquitos?"

"They're not bothering anyone yet. Were you bitten while you were out?"

"No, but you just want me to feel exposed. Right?"

He gave me a broad smile, all sharp, white teeth. "Yes, Jenny. That's right."

"Why?"

"Because it turns me on to humble you, to have you serve my whims. I want you to know that I would use you anyway I like, anywhere I like. Or you can say no right now. We'll forget this whole thing."

I hesitated for a moment, but I wanted Juan to do anything he wanted to me. I was curious about how it might feel to be punished and fucked hard outside in the open. Even if we were alone, the birds and frogs and other critters would see. Somehow, that made the whole thing more exciting to me.

Plus, it really *was* hot in the house after being closed for hours while the sun shone down on the tarp and what remained of the roof.

I waddled out to the patio. The beach shoes were definitely not sexy, so I asked Juan if I could take them off and he agreed. He'd swept up nicely the day before, when restoring the patio to order, so it was safe for me to be barefoot.

Juan pointed with the paddle to a white painted wrought iron love seat on the patio opposite the table where we'd had our dinner the night before. He had replaced the thick, brightly colored canvas flower cushions on the patio set, but I didn't sit down. I got the sense that wasn't what he wanted.

"Take off your towel, kneel on the seat cushions and hold on to the back of the seat," he commanded.

I folded my towel over the back of the loveseat so I could grip something other than the hard metal curlicues of the seat's back. Juan took off his towel and tossed it beside me on the thick cushion, along with the packs of condoms, and stood to my left, lightly tapping my butt with the paddle.

"This is really going to hurt, Jenny," he warned. "Remind me why you are being punished."

"Because I left the house this morning without letting you know and I got lost and only ran into you by dumb luck."

He stroked my bare back, running the tip of the paddle down my spine. "No. That's not why."

I took a deep breath as the paddle returned to tap the fullness of my cheeks. I guessed again, "Because I got drunk and wound up trapped here with you for this whole thing."

"No." Juan tapped me twice, gently, right at the center of my butt.

"It can't be the beer. You already spanked me with the spoon for that."

"It's not the beer, Jenny." Two more light taps. "Tell me why."

"Because I asked for this?"

"That's right. It's what you wanted. I'm going to give you what you asked for and then you can decide whether you ever want it again."

"Okay." I nodded, drops of water from my damp hair trickling down my back and over my face.

"I want you to count out each swat," Juan said.

"How many am I getting?"

"As many as it takes to turn your ass cherry red, or until I'm satisfied that you've had enough."

"Okay."

With that simple word, I gave in to my need for pain and punishment, something I'd never really been able to satisfy except by putting my life at risk through poor decision making. When the first swat of Juan's paddle made contact with my flesh, it sounded like a balloon popping, and felt like fire. The pain reached deep into my butt muscles, radiating down my thighs to my toes and up my spine to the roots of my hair. I felt the heat building up as he continued and cried out the numbers as each successive swat tenderized my rear. By the time I reached fifteen, I was sure my butt had to be bright red, but Juan kept going.

"Stop, please," I sobbed, instead of saying twenty. "I'm sorry, I can't anymore."

"You're only pink, little one."

"But it really hurts!"

"I told you it would."

"Yes, but…"

Pop. Pop. Pop. Juan landed three more swats in swift succession, and I rebelled, jumping from the seat to stand on my feet and protect my backside.

"No more," I wept. "That was enough. I swear. I learned my lesson."

"That's not the lesson." Juan put the paddle down on the seat, and approached me slowly, to caress my tear stained cheek. "That's just the warmup. Are you sure you can handle the rest?"

"No more paddling?"

"No more paddling, but if you do something so stupid again, leaving the house without a plan, I won't stop until you shine bright apple red, even if I have to tie you down to do it. Do you understand?"

"Yes, sir."

"Good, now sit down."

"What? I can't sit like this!"

"You have to."

"But my butt hurts like hell!"

"There are cushions on the seat. Sit down, Jenny Banks." He ran his thumb along my lips. "I'm going to fuck this sweet little mouth now."

Even with the cushions, though, sitting was torture. My butt burned and the rough canvas scratched, as did the nasty little hard canvas covered buttons of the quilting. I winced when I sat on those, and Juan grinned as he stood before me, both his massive legs locking mine together, his erection right up against my face.

"Open your mouth for me, baby," he commanded, threading his fingers through my damp hair with one hand as he stroked his dick with the other.

"It's a lot," I said, unsure how I could handle a cock this large.

"I know. Take as much of it as you can."

I wrapped my lips around the tip, sucking his sweet, salty pre-cum, and he pushed in further, gripping my hair to keep my head where he wanted it.

"Relax that jaw, baby," he said. "I won't choke you today."

Today? Did he intend to choke me another time? Somehow, that sounded promising instead of threatening. After all, if he planned to choke me another day, maybe he'd do other things another day, too. I forgot briefly about my aching ass, enthralled by the feel of his hard length against my tongue and my lips as he thrust slowly in and out of my mouth. He reached the back, but went no further. I wouldn't gag if he pushed. Maybe I'd tell him that next time. I enjoyed the clean, manly scent of his skin so close to my nose and thrilled at the burning gaze he gave when I looked up into those dark eyes. His expression told me he was getting more pleasure out of this than he had thought. Juan sped up his strokes, still keeping my head captive with one hand while holding the base of his shaft in his other fist. When he was ready to go over the edge, he pulled out of my mouth and stroked himself the rest of the way to spurt his cum on my face.

"Lick it all up, baby," he said, letting go of my hair and slapping my right breast. "Never waste a drop of my cum."

I made a show of it, collecting his semen delicately with the tips of my fingers and then sucking each one of them with a delighted pop of my lips, as if I'd just eaten my favorite meal. Juan approved, bending to kiss my lips gently, then growing more demanding until his kiss left me breathless and hungry for him. I was sure I would leave a stain on the fabric of the patio cushion whenever I stood up again, assuming my legs would still hold me up.

When he finally released my lips, he was growing hard again. "Stand up now, precious, and put your hands up against the wall."

I smiled and did as he asked, standing against the wall as if he were a cop about to frisk me. Instead of frisking me though, he gripped both my wrists in his right hand, putting them up over my head, and started spanking me with his left hand so hard I went up on tiptoes, wailing. My butt hadn't come close to recovering from the paddle, and it had endured the cushion with only the distraction of Juan's dick, making me somewhat numb to the pain. His delicious kiss had briefly made me forget all about my derriere, but now he was literally lighting my ass on fire again. I couldn't get away because he had my hands pressed against the wall and he stood so close. I wept and wailed with each strike, begging him to stop, but he was enjoying himself too much raining hellfire on me. "When I say you're going to be punished, Chiquita, that's what's going to happen," he growled in my ear. "Got it?"

"Yes," I sobbed. My breasts scratched against the wall as Juan pressed himself against me.

He dipped his fingers between my lower lips, stroking my pulsing pussy, soothing the ache in my core which was every bit as intense as the ache in my ass. He kept stroking me until I was whimpering and panting, raising my ass and parting my legs to give him better access. Then he stepped away and left me breathing heavily against the wall, unsure of what to expect. I looked over to the love seat where he'd gone to open a condom packet. He returned to me, slipped the condom on and slid his thick cock into me with a punishing thrust, grabbing my hips and pounding me against the wall so hard that I was sure he bruised my cervix. I was sweating and sighing and not minding for a minute each time his hard pelvis hit my heated back cheeks. I loved every second of Juan's hard fuck, although maybe he was bruising my vagina, because of it. Then he pulled out and parted my back cheeks, stroking my sphincter with the tip of his penis, which was slick with my fluids.

"I don't think I can take it," I said, breathless.

I'd been fucked in the ass before, but never like this and never by such a large man. "You can take it," Juan said as he pressed the broad head of his dick through the pucker, stretching me slowly as he fitted more of his length into my back passage. I'd never felt so much pressure, and yet it also felt good. Juan took his time letting me adjust. Just as I was relaxing into it, he filled me all the way, pushing in the rest of his length with a heavy grunt and a quick thrust, so that his pelvis smacked me again. I was so full I thought I would pop. He remained inside, unmoving, as his right hand gripped the back of my neck and the other reached around to squeeze my breast, pinching my sensitive, hardened nipple. I whimpered, then gasped when Juan pressed me up against the wall, the rough stucco bruising my cheek. He began pumping me hard. I struggled to keep my balance on my toes, pinned by his cock in my ass, his left hand digging into my hip. He leaned in to hiss in my ear. "Bad girls get whipped and fucked hard in the ass, and you... are... a *very... bad... girl.*"

That probably shouldn't have turned me on, but it did. I moaned with each hard pump. The only problem was I needed him to let me finish. I hung on the edge. My pussy throbbed and my core pinched, and my clit ached so much it brought tears to my eyes. I needed him to touch me or let me touch myself.

After he came in my ass, Juan pulled out and spanked my pussy. I was so very close and each violent strike on my folds felt like a kiss and each time his rough fingers struck the knot of nerves in my clit. My breath caught. I screeched, but he parted my legs wider so his fingers really hit their mark. The rough attention ignited my vulva and spread heat through my body to the very tips of my fingers and toes. When he struck me again, I almost broke from the intensity of sensations rocking my body, a blend of ache and delight I'd never sampled until that day. "Oh, Daddy, *please,*" I screeched, surprising myself. I'd never called a man that during sex and wasn't sure I wanted a daddy, but it just seemed appropriate.

"I'm not your daddy, slut." Juan slipped three fingers into my channel as his thumb pressed into my sore pucker. "I'm your nightmare."

I didn't think so. This felt like a dream, maybe a rough one, but a good one. As he pumped me harder with his hand,

I crashed under the wave of an orgasm so violent, it rocked my whole body. I moaned with such a loud, broken shudder it must have sounded as if I was just cleaved in two by an axe. And I *was* being torn asunder as Juan's thick fingers kept penetrating my vagina, which his oversized dick had already turned to mush. His thumb breached the bruised petals of my rose. I was riding his hand, whether or not I liked it. But I liked it plenty.

I came for him a second time, this time harder. When my knees buckled, Juan's body and his hand held me up. He kept pumping. Though I was sure I couldn't come again, he released my neck and trapped my right hand in his large hand, reaching around my front, his fingers pressing my fingers to pinch my clit. "Come for me, baby. Prove to me you're sorry for being such a bad girl."

And I did. I came like a rocket launch at Kennedy, so hard I heard the roaring of the thrusters and felt the wind whip up around us.

"Fuck!" Juan shouted, taking his hand out of me and pressing me completely against the wall covered by his body. Then he whispered in my ear, "Run inside. Go to the office and shut the door. Don't come out until I tell you."

"What?" I asked, but he was already stepping back and slinging me towards the sliding glass doors. I noticed the wind was real and had intensified. There was a deafening swatting and swishing sound as the military helicopter descended above the broken jungle only fifty feet away.

Shit!

Chapter 11

What the actual fuck did I get myself into?

I DIDN'T HESITATE to hide as Juan commanded. After all, I was stark naked and what clothing I had was somewhere unreachable at this point. After I was in the office, my mind rushed to process the scene I'd glimpsed only briefly.

Why was there a military helicopter landing on Juan's lawn?

He hadn't followed me inside, so I figured two things. One, he didn't give a shit who saw him naked, which was bold of him. I mean, the man looked amazing naked. He had nothing to hide. Two, he knew why they were there, or at least he had some idea. Maybe it was a rescue and supply mission coordinated by FEMA, or whatever. If so, their timing sucked. They could have come ten minutes later. Maybe I would have had some clothes on by then, or at least had one more orgasm. I would have come again if Juan kept pumping.

God, I was sore. I really felt it when I sat on the couch I'd been sleeping on when Juan first found me. Everything below my waist pulsed with pain and tingled with pleasure. I stood up again and paced around the small room, wondering what came next. After a while, I heard male voices in the den, not just Juan's, and pressed myself against the door to listen.

"Fine, I'll do what you want, but you've got to take this girl back somewhere safe. She's lost here and I can't leave her alone waiting for me to be done."

And here's the crazy thing. I completely disregarded my instructions and my best interest at this point.

"No," I said, coming out naked into the den, where Juan stood, still stark naked, arguing with an older man in an army uniform with a beret on his head. "I'm not leaving."

"You get back inside!" Juan barked.

"No, I will not." I held my ground, though the sergeant, or whatever he was, was trying really hard, and failing, to get his eyes off my tits. "I'm not leaving the house empty. Someone should be here to protect it if you're leaving."

"It's none of your goddamned business, Jenny Banks!" Juan raised his voice even louder. "This is your chance to go home."

"I don't have a home."

"Don't be ridiculous." Juan turned to the older man. "Can you arrange flight ops for her to Reading, Pennsylvania? That's where her family is. They must be worried about her."

"No, they're not!"

"I've got enough on my hands without dealing with whatever this shit is," the older man said to Juan.

"If you want this job done, get her to Pennsylvania. Today."

"Fine. I'll take you both now and get her on a separate

flight. But we have to go, *now*, and she can't go looking like that."

"Put on your dress and your heels, Jenny," Juan commanded.

"I don't even know where they are at this point! I think all my stuff blew away. And I don't *want* to go home."

Next thing I knew, Juan draped me over his shoulder, my head bobbing against his firm naked rear, as he carried me over to the walk-in closet in the master bedroom. When he put me down again, he grabbed a pair of torn fatigues and a t-shirt and threw them at me, while he rushed to dress himself in full fatigues like he was setting off for war. He looked amazing in those.

"Get dressed, Jenny Banks," he growled.

"I don't want to go to Pennsylvania, Juan Ruiz." I was not dressing. "And where are *you* going? *Why* are you going? Who *is* that out there? Why do you have a *fucking military helicopter* in your backyard?"

"I am a killer, Jenny Banks." He buckled his belt. "They need someone dead. It's that simple. Now, get dressed. Go be with your mother and father. They need you."

"Why can't I just stay here and watch the house until you come back from killing whomever?"

"Because I don't want you here, Jenny. I want you gone. I want you not to be my problem anymore."

"Well, I want to be your problem a while longer," I said. "That all felt magnificent, just now, before the helicopter arrived. Didn't you enjoy it?"

"Jenny, I fucked you, which was all I said I would do. I promised nothing else, other than to keep you safe through this hurricane, which I also did. It's going to be a long time before the world is right again. I can't leave you alone in a wrecked house lost in the middle of nowhere. Okay? I wasn't expecting to be called out, but this is a lucky break for both of us. You need to go. Now."

"The person you're going to kill, are they bad?"

"Everybody's bad, Jenny. Especially you. Get dressed!"

"Can you at least give me a kiss first, one of your dangerous kisses? If it's going to be my last, make it a deadly one."

Juan stared at me for a while, then approached me slowly. I backed up, forcing him to keep walking before he could reach me, until he pressed my back up against the wall of his closet. He knew what I needed without me having to say it. He put his hand around my throat, just as he had when he found me nosing through his things.

"Is this what you want, rag doll?" He brought his face right up to mine. His breath was fire on my cheeks. "Do you want your Master to keep taking you, punishing you, breaking your soft little body, using you up, making you beg for more?" He brushed my lips with his own, only teasing at a kiss. "Is that what you need, my naughty… little… slut?"

I smiled. "Yes, please."

He kissed me hard, pressing himself against my naked body, grabbing one of my breasts in his hand and one of my hands with the other, our fingers intertwined as our tongues wrestled and our breath quickened and Juan's hard cock pressed against my bare belly through the rough military fabric between us. I was lost in that kiss for what felt like forever, and yet never long enough. As soon as he broke away, I felt hollow, like the world really had ended and it could never be put right again.

"If you still feel that way after the recovery is over," he whispered against my lips, "then stop by here. But you'd better be a good girl between now and then. No drinking. No parties. No other men. And you'd better know for a fact that you're not leaving if I ever catch you in my house again."

"Okay."

"Now, get dressed, Jenny. I've got people to kill, and no time."

"What's going to happen to the house?"

"I do not know at this point. Doesn't matter. Can't be helped."

I could tell Juan was upset about it, though he was resigned to do his duty, whatever that was. I felt I should do the same, so I put on the torn fatigues and t-shirt and the silly beach shoes which made me look like a clown, then followed Juan back to the den where the sergeant waited impatient and angry.

"Jesus Christ," the man spat. "Doesn't she have any clothes at all?"

"There's been a hurricane here, if you haven't noticed," I snapped.

Juan swatted my ass pretty hard. It was already very tender, so I yipped. "Show respect, and shut the fuck up."

Juan took some time to lock up the weapons he had pulled out for our protection and place them back in the safe he kept in the small office. Then he did a cursory turn around the house, like he was saying goodbye. Finally resolved to his fate, he nodded and followed the sergeant out the back door.

I followed the two men quietly to the helicopter after that. Juan helped me get over the fallen trunks, which would have been difficult with my clown beach shoes on. Then he lifted me up into the cabin of the helicopter where it really hurt to sit on the flat seat. He didn't say another word to me or to the sergeant all the way to Eglin Air Force Base near Pensacola, where they were apparently coordinating the recovery effort. The place was bustling. Juan had a flight to catch right away, to wherever he needed to go next, but he stopped to kiss me before we parted. "I meant it, Jenny

Banks," he said. "If you ever cast a shadow on my door again, you'll live to regret it." The brief but passionate kiss, coupled with his threat and his wicked grin, made me feel all sorts of wonderful.

"You don't have a door."

"I'll build another. Go now, little one. Your mother and father need you. I don't."

He didn't give me a chance to argue with him. He just turned his back on me and marched off. A young airman came up to me, to take me to the plane which would fly me back to Pennsylvania. I didn't go right away, though. I watched as Juan made his way down the tarmac to the C-130 aircraft he boarded to go kill someone somewhere. I hoped he'd turn around before vanishing up the ramp into its belly, but he didn't give me a second look. I probably shouldn't have cared. After all, who was he to me?

Nobody.

"Don't worry, ma'am," the airman said, passing me a small pack of tissues from his pocket. "Your man will be just fine. He's a pro. Now let's get you on your plane so you can get home to your folks."

Nobody had ever called me ma'am before and for some weird reason, I liked it. I smiled and thanked him through tears and sniffles.

Then I sobbed a river on my private flight up to Reading.

"What in heaven's name are you wearing?" My mother always focused on what mattered most. She went back into the kitchen, where she started the blender to make herself a pitcher of margaritas. It was late, almost midnight, and I was too tired to argue with her.

"Things were pretty bad in Florida, Mother. This was all I had."

"So, why are you home? Are you just quitting college without getting your masters?"

"No, I..." I shook my head. I shouldn't have expected her to remember my call. "I came home because a hurricane turned my college upside down, along with the rest of South Florida. Thousands of people are homeless right now. The roads are ruined. There are no utilities. It's a mess."

"Still, that's a strange outfit."

"Yeah, it was all a friend had available when they came to rescue us."

"What friend of yours would wear clothes like that?"

"A good friend. He helped me survive."

"*He?*"

"Yes, Mother."

"Okay," she shrugged, filling a large tumbler with crushed ice margarita. "Do you want one?"

"No. I'll just have some water." They'd given me water on the flight over, and the driver they'd arranged for me had another bottle waiting for me in the back seat when he met me at the airport, but I was still thirsty and hot, and exhausted. "Then I'm going to take a long shower and go to bed."

"Okay, have fun." Mom took her tumbler out to the back patio, as well as the pitcher from the blender. She might fall asleep out there and it wouldn't make a difference. It wasn't my problem, anyway. I'd learned a long time ago that I couldn't beg or persuade my mother to stop drinking. At some point, I'd found it easier to ignore her, or to join her.

I had no intention of joining her, though. After all, I'd promised Juan that I wouldn't drink.

Our house was too big for us. It had always been cavernous and hollow. My great grandfather had built it to prove his wealth, but he had six children. By the time it passed over to my grandfather, it was already too much house for them. They only had two children. Except, my grandmother entertained a lot, so they got better use out of the rooms.

My mother tried to do that, at first, but she lacked whatever it takes to be a good society hostess. Sobriety isn't necessarily a requirement, but some ability to hide your disdain for people probably helps.

Even before Dad's breakdown, the house felt haunted. I used to spend hours lost in the various empty rooms, looking for family treasure in the large dusty attic, exploring the dark recesses of the basement. For many years, I believed I was exploring the house with a little boy named Peter, who nobody else knew about. My mom said he was just my imaginary friend, and maybe that's all he was. But when I told my dad one day about playing with Peter, he went white as a sheet and insisted I stop lying. I learned later, from Mom, that Dad had an uncle named Peter, who drowned in our pool when he was ten. I looked for pictures in an old family album to see if I recognized the boy, but there was no record of him ever existing. Apparently, my great-grandmother had destroyed all the family photos in which her dead first son appeared. Anyway, I hadn't seen Peter in years. If he was still in the house somewhere, he'd got bored with me.

The house wasn't a complete mess, which was a relief. We had a full-time live-in housekeeper for a while, but when she quit, Mom decided she didn't want to replace her. Instead, she hired a cleaning service who came around twice a month. That worked well enough. Even on a bender, there was only so much mess a woman alone would make.

My bedroom was exactly as I had left it during my last visit, over Christmas. My drawers and closet were full of comfortable, fashionable clothes and right-sized shoes. I slipped off the clown shoes right away, and slipped my feet into my blue terrycloth slippers, took off the fatigues and shirt, taking a deep breath of the fabric to capture the lingering scent of Juan.

I knew I shouldn't be worrying about him. Whatever he was doing, he knew how to do it. Plus, he never wanted to see me again. Not technically, anyway. Though he had said if I went back to him, I could stay.

I was under the shower, enjoying the luxury of hot water on my skin and sore muscles, when it suddenly occurred to me I did not know how to find my way back to Juan's house. I didn't even know the address. I'd been so drunk when I drove there at night that I'd have no way to recognize the roads I took, even after the clean-up. I figured I could look him up online.

As soon as I got out of the shower, I wrapped myself in my fluffy blue bathrobe, rushed over to my desk, and turned on my computer. An hour later, I still couldn't find any trace of Juan Ruiz. It was as if he didn't exist. I could almost tell myself I imagined him, except my butt was still really sore from that paddling and the spanking that followed and the rest of it. And I'd seen him get into that cargo plane. I was sure of that. I still had the tissues the nice airman, Marcus, gave me on the tarmac. I had Juan's torn fatigues, his t-shirt and his stupid beach shoes. When I closed my eyes, I could still taste his minty mouth, and I could feel his soft, full lips on mine. No, I hadn't dreamt up Juan. He wasn't a ghost like Peter. I hadn't made him up. He was very real, and he was really gone.

But Juan had tricked me. He had to have known he was unlisted and invisible, and that my chances of ever finding him again were slim to none. Well, I'll tell you one thing for free. I don't give up that easily.

Chapter 12

Getting my shit in order took longer than I liked.

I SPENT the next few days checking in on those of my friends who had functioning phones. Not all of them did, but the university had done a good job of restoring power to the dorms, which were unaffected by the storm, so I could reach Gillian and Maggie. They didn't seem at all surprised to learn that I was in Pennsylvania and had assumed I flew out ahead of Hank.

Maggie was shocked to hear that I had stayed at the party house during the storm, but she couldn't remember the name of the guys who had invited me to the party.

"I told you not to go," she said. Maggie loved being right.

"Well it was a good thing. The only problem is that I can't remember exactly where I was."

"Why does it matter at this point?"

"Well, the guy who owns the house helped me get out, and I wanted to thank him."

"Well, just look him up. It's not that hard."

"Yeah, you're right."

I would not tell Maggie more about Juan than I needed to. I was really grateful that she didn't think to ask me how Juan had flown me out of Florida. I didn't think Juan would want me telling people he was some sort of special ops sniper. It sounded ridiculous. She wouldn't believe me, anyway. I hardly believed it myself.

The rest of the time I spent on mundane things, recovering my lost IDs and credit cards, following the online courses the university had set up for students who weren't able to get back to campus, and hiring a private detective to help me track Juan down.

It was a bit of a desperate move and risky if Juan really wanted to stay off the radar, but I needed some clue of where to find him, because I was definitely going back.

At the end of the month, Mom and I drove out to visit Dad at the Silver Valley Residence where he'd been committed for his latest one-hundred and twenty day stretch. Something had set him off after I last saw him at home, during the Christmas break. He hadn't kept up with his medications, so he'd had to be committed again in April. I hoped he might be lucid and ready to come home soon. I loved my father. He was a gentle man, frail, but incredibly creative. Dad had been a talented engineer, once, but that wasn't really his passion. He was an artist and a storyteller, a gifted illustrator. Dad's dark comic book series Earth2X, had done pretty well and had actually helped grow the fortune my grandfather had left us. The problem was, Dad got lost in his fictional worlds sometimes. The lines blurred between the plots of his serial comics and real life. He'd learned to hide when he was in a decline, locking himself up in his art room. Mom never tried to get him out of there. She left him alone to get lost in the fog, in the big empty house, a living ghost.

In fairness to her, Dad's illness was a lot to deal with. Even someone who wasn't a malignant narcissist would have had a hard time adapting to his low points when we lost him to his voices and hallucinations. She had her own problems. But if she cared at all about another human being, then she should have cared for Dad. He gave her the world, but it wasn't enough.

We went to the residence together, and shortly after we both greeted Dad, Mom left to go have a cigarette. She didn't come back. Dad looked good, under the circumstances, though a little on the thin side. His thick brown hair went gray the year before, just a light dusting, but now his temples were frosted, as were his sideburns. He had shaved, or the staff had shaved him, and his hair was trim and neat. He wore the Institute's neat navy jogging suit and white canvas shoes.

Dad unwrapped my birthday gift as eagerly as a boy on Christmas morning and smiled when he found a first-edition copy of *A Clockwork Orange*. I'd found it for him through a local bookseller in Reading who Dad first introduced me to years ago. It might not be the best book for his current state, but I knew he loved it. He deserved to have something he loved nearby every day.

"Where have you been, ladybug?" he asked, when we sat together at the little table of his private suite. The residence was a good place, the best money could buy, almost like a hotel, except Dad couldn't check out whenever he wanted. "I couldn't find you in the house."

"I know, Dad, I was in college, in Miami. Remember? I just came home for your birthday, then I'm going back."

"Do you really like it there?"

I thought about it. The Hank-pocalypse aside, I had grown fond of South Florida—especially of one of its residents. I intended to find Juan again, which meant never leaving.

I nodded and smiled. "Yes, Dad, I do. I think I'll stay after college."

"I'll miss you if you don't come back. The house isn't the same when you're not there."

I put my hand on his. It trembled under my fingers. "I promise I'll always come home to visit."

Dad gave me a weak smile, but he avoided my eyes. "Your mother misses you, too."

"No, she doesn't, Dad, but that's okay. You and me, remember? Inseparable, no matter what comes."

It was something he'd said after he got out the first time they committed him, after the incident at the zoo. Dad felt so bad for leaving me alone. He wept as he promised it would never happen again. Of course, it had, but he couldn't help it.

Dad nodded and sighed as he looked out the window. I wasn't sure whether he could see my mother smoking in the back garden. I mean, she was there, but I never knew what he saw when he looked at her. At some point, he'd created a fiction around his wife which made loving her bearable to him. I would not change his story.

"If I die, you get everything, you know." He spoke barely above a whisper. "She has an allowance, but it's all yours."

"Dad, please don't talk about dying. You just turned fifty-seven. You're still young."

He looked out the window again, but I still wasn't sure what he saw. "It could happen any time."

"Are you taking your medication?"

"Yes, they make sure of that." He turned his intense gaze on me. "I feel wrong, you know. I mean, the voices are quiet, and I'm calm, but I'm tired."

"Dad, I need you to promise me you'll keep up with your meds when you get out."

He nodded. "Yes, ladybug." I didn't believe him, though, and I was worried.

I decided that I had to take more active measures to ensure Dad didn't go off the rails again.

After I left Dad, I stopped to see his doctor and asked about getting a live-in nurse to look after him at home. The doctor told me there was a nurse already at the residence with whom my father got along well—Burt Summers—who might be interested in the job. Dr. Fields said we lived closer to Burt's parents, who were getting older, so he wouldn't have to worry as much about being a two hour drive away if they needed him. The advantage was that Dad trusted Burt even when he was having episodes. Dr. Fields warned me it wouldn't be cheap, but I thought it was more than worth the expense, if I could be sure that Dad wasn't alone after I was gone.

The doctor arranged for Burt and me to meet in his office. Mom was still out somewhere in the gardens, apparently smoking an entire carton of cigarettes. I liked Burt right away. He was a large guy, of gentle demeanor, quiet, and a good listener. He heard me out on the offer to move in permanently in our house, so he could be sure Dad wouldn't get lost in there. I told him he could bring his parents to live there with him if he wanted. We had plenty of room. He turned me down on that offer, saying his parents loved their home and they wouldn't want to live anywhere else.

I know it sounds weird, but that made me miss Juan, reminding me about how much he loved his childhood home —enough to rebuild it when it was taken away. I still didn't feel that way about my house, and I probably never would. It was my great-grandfather's legacy and nothing to me but a showy display of wealth. Worst of all, it was haunted. I didn't mention the ghost of Peter to Burt, though. Maybe they'd never run into each other.

We came to an agreement for Burt to come home with my father when he got released from the residence in the third week of August. I didn't enjoy having to wait so long to go back to find Juan, but South Florida still wasn't straightened out. There was no point in my flying down until I had half a chance of getting around.

Mom was livid about my decision. She thought having another person in the house would interfere with how she wanted to live her life. We argued all the way back. I finally shut her down by reminding her she was always free to divorce my father and move out on her own.

By the time Dad and Burt arrived, I was more than ready to go. I'd had my fill of my mother's passive aggressive attempts to get back at me for ruining her fun. Her constant drinking was a problem, too. I came close to having a few drinks myself several times. Only my promise to Juan kept me from doing that.

Speaking of Juan, the detective I'd hired to find him had come up empty. Actually, that wasn't entirely true. He came to me with a warning to stop searching. "Some people shouldn't be found for a reason." He wouldn't tell me who had warned him off the search, but he cut his fee in half.

I hung around another week, just to be sure that Burt settled in well. Funny enough, after a couple of days, my mother was all sweetness and light around him. Whatever the reason for that, it seemed they'd all settled into a life that would hold. I promised Dad I'd be back to visit him for Christmas, and he seemed happy with that. Having Burt around to keep him company was really helping, and Burt was an excellent cook to boot, so Dad was eating better.

I said nothing to Dad about bringing Juan with me when

I came home for the holidays. After all, I'd have to find Juan first, then convince him it was a good idea.

I was really anxious as I boarded my plane in Philadelphia, even though I'd done everything possible to leave things settled at home. I still had to replace my flyaway car. The insurance had paid me for the lost one and I planned to stop by the dealership the next day. I'd heard from Maggie that the parts of Miami around my university were open for business now. I still wanted to find Juan, and I did not know where to start. The warning from the detective I'd hired had zero impact on me. He might not want to go any further, but I would do anything to be back in Juan's arms.

On the flight down, I fell asleep, and I dreamt about the first morning I saw the destruction, making my piles and sorting things out. When I woke up, I remembered the mailbox—Kensington sixty-three. It was as close as I might come to a lead. There were probably many Kensingtons in South Florida, but probably not a lot of them who also lived in South Dade at a house with the number 63.

It surprised me I hadn't thought of it sooner. Even if the mailbox had traveled in the wind, it wouldn't have come from very far. I just had to find the Kensingtons and I would find Juan again.

Then I just had to figure out the rest.

No, I still didn't believe that I loved Juan. How could I? I still hardly knew him. And what was love, anyway? But I lusted desperately after him. That hadn't changed with him sending me away. He was my last thought at night and my first thought in the morning, and my constant thought during the quiet moments of my day. I wanted him to be my lover, my cruel master. I wanted to feel his hard hand and his gentle embrace. I wanted to kiss those lips and suck that cock. I needed to bite him and lick him all over, and I needed him to do the same to me, out in the open in the backyard, no matter who saw.

No other man would do. If I couldn't have him… Well, it would not come to that, I told myself.

I really believed it.

Chapter 13

Maggie and Gillian have opinions, and I have to go to the zoo.

MIAMI INTERNATIONAL AIRPORT was back up and running just fine, and almost as crowded as usual. I got a taxi to get down to my dorms at Waterside Village in Coral Gables, where I lived with Maggie and Gillian. I could easily have afforded to have a single apartment dorm, but I hadn't wanted one. The whole point of going to college at Miami University was that I wanted to feel like a normal person and make new friends. That was the original idea, anyway. It turns out that when you're not really comfortable trusting people, all you can make are friendly acquaintances.

As far as roommates go, Maggie and Gillian were the best I'd had so far in college. Maggie studied medicine, so she was usually in her room with her books, but when she came out, she was really in the mood to party. Gillian was more in touch with nature. She wandered in and out and was usually gone during the weekends on some expedition or other in the

Everglades. Gillian was friendly and fun to hang out with, though she was a little shy around men. She rarely joined us when Maggie and I went partying with Maggie and my mutual friends. Gillian was more sensible than Maggie and me, but I liked them both well enough.

Still, they got on my nerves almost right away when I came back, mainly because they peppered me with questions. The three of us sat in the living room of our apartment, enjoying some frozen pizza Gillian had heated in the oven and a few beers. Water for me, though. I insisted.

They wanted to know how I'd got to Pennsylvania if I was stuck going through hurricane Hank somewhere I couldn't remember with a man I didn't know.

I was reluctant to breach Juan's confidence and had enough sense to know he wouldn't want me telling people what had happened. The warning from the detective I'd hired had reinforced that notion. So, in the end I lied. I told them I had reached out to my family, and they had sent a rescue team for me. Gillian pointed out it didn't explain why I didn't know where I had been, since they had to have found me to take me away. I just said that I was so disoriented myself that I couldn't recall and they'd found me using some GPS coordinates Juan had given them, but I had forgotten.

"It's just weird," Gillian noted, not really buying into my story. "But it's good you got out. It hasn't been easy here."

"Well, you had power and water right away," I noted.

"Yes, but it's been hard to get gas and you couldn't really get far from campus. I haven't been able to get out to the Everglades in weeks."

"We're all going a little stir-crazy," Maggie added, reaching for another slice of pizza. "We put on a few parties here in the complex, you know, to take the edge off. But now that you're back, we have to figure out what's open. Some clubs on SoBe are wrecked. There's nothing much going on out there, but there are still places to go in Fort Lauderdale."

"I'm not back to party, Maggie," I said. "I'm done with that."

"Seriously? Were your parents furious with you for getting drunk and winding up who knows where during a hurricane?"

"I'm just over it, is all."

Maggie laughed like she didn't believe me. "Okay, then. So, what are your plans?"

"Well, first I'm going to get a car to replace the one I lost. Other than that, I'm going to get back to classes and catch up on what I've missed."

"Haven't you been keeping up online?" Gillian asked.

"Some, but it's not the same."

"Well, I think it's good that you're settling in to study," she said. "You always do well, but if you focus, you could graduate next year and be done."

"Yes, Mother," I teased.

"Sorry," she shrugged. "Anyway, I forgot to tell you my great news. I finally got a paid internship!"

I was especially happy for Gillian since she had to pay her own way through school and it wasn't cheap. "That's great! Where?"

"At the Miami Zoo. They have a mess there right now and need all the help they can get. I get credits too, so it's a double-win, and I'm working with the reptiles who have had a very hard time. Some of them are spooked."

"Oh, wow, what a coincidence," I said.

"What do you mean?"

"The guy I stayed with during the hurricane said he worked at the zoo, too. Some kind of caretaker, I think. You haven't run across him, have you? Juan Ruiz?"

Gillian put her slice of pizza down, she paled, and her

brown eyes opened up like two large plates. "Oh my God. That was *him*?"

I felt myself blushing. "Yep."

"He's not a caretaker, Jenny. He's…" Gillian tried to find a word for it, but apparently she couldn't. She just shook her head. "He's the…" But Gillian couldn't finish.

"The *what*?" Maggie pushed.

"He's like security. He's the one who trains the guns team, and he's the one they send out to kill any really dangerous animals that pose a danger to the community."

"Oh, that makes sense," I said, without thinking. I probably should have acted more surprised. I *was* surprised to hear that Gillian had met Juan. More than surprised. My heart beat faster and I had a lump in my throat. Until that moment, I'd just assumed he'd come back from his mission. But suddenly, I realized, I was incredibly relieved to know for a fact that he was still alive. That he was real. I hadn't imagined him. Someone else I knew had met him, and she evidently hated him.

"Why?" Maggie asked, after Gillian went apoplectic.

I shrugged. "I know he had guns in the house, in case of any looters. He said he could shoot."

"He's an *asshole*," Gillian said, making a face.

"Yeah," I laughed.

"No, seriously, he's *completely* antisocial," Gillian said, obviously annoyed that I was making light of it. "There is something wrong with that man."

"Uh-huh." I nodded, still smiling.

Gillian shook her head, then went on, apparently thinking that I needed to understand the depth of Juan's wrongness. "He wanted to train me to shoot! They have a certain number of the staff who are qualified to carry guns in case an animal becomes dangerous on the premises. I was like, no. I told him it's against my principles to use a gun. He just snorted. Then he said I didn't belong in the zoo if I couldn't handle security protocols. How does that even make sense? We're supposed to be *taking care* of the animals, not *killing* them."

"Well, I guess the point is to defend people from the animals if anything goes wrong," I said. "They are *wild* animals, Gillian."

"That's not the point. The point is how he acted toward me, like he was superior or something. Like there was something wrong with *me* for not wanting to learn how to shoot."

"Hmm." I took a long drink of water. It probably would not be wise for me to say anything else or try to defend Juan. He *was* a bossy, irascible asshole. That's what I… No. Not that. Well, that's what I very much *liked* about him. Still, at least I knew he was back at the zoo. Safe. Alive. Pissing people off. I was smiling too much, and I couldn't really stop myself.

The conversation moved away from Juan almost right away. Maggie tried to clear some of the tension coming from Gillian's side of the small living room by catching me up on the current state of her colorful love life. She had been juggling three boyfriends—medical students like she was— and she had somehow talked all three men into having a menage. It hadn't happened yet, but she was definitely looking forward to it.

"We could make it five," Maggie suggested. "The guys are really cool. You know Josh already. You know he's hot. But trust me, Kevin and Matt are even hotter. Matt is definitely your type—a real party animal—from a very wealthy New York family, stocks or something. They have a winter house in Palm Beach. He's a catch."

"No, thank you. I'm not really up to that much action."

"Geez! You don't drink, you don't want to party and you're not interested in having an exciting romp with three very sexy and very eligible bachelors? What happened to you in Pennsylvania, Jenny?"

Maggie was only partially teasing. I could understand if she was a little sore. After all, we'd been partners in vice since we first met. It was usually Maggie trying to talk me out of my most dangerous impulses. The worst part is that I couldn't really tell her why I had suddenly changed, because the truth was patently ridiculous.

After all, I wasn't sure I could find Juan's house again. Even if I showed up at his door, he might just tell me to go away. And I only knew him briefly. That short stretch of time we spent together—going through the hurricane and dealing with the aftermath—had been intense, but I had no good reason to stop drinking and sleeping with other guys just because Juan said I should.

I couldn't explain it all to Maggie. I wasn't sure myself why I felt it was important. For whatever reason, I cared what Juan thought of me. I wanted to prove to him I was better than he thought, stronger than he imagined.

I'd never given a damn what people thought of me. So why did I care what Juan thought? Because he'd seen right through my shit and called me out on it. No one had bothered to do that before he came along.

"Well?" Maggie asked, noting my hesitation. I'd got lost in my head trying to figure out if there was any way to explain that didn't make me sound ridiculous.

"I just… I'm not playing anymore," I said with a shrug. "It's like Gillian said. I'm almost done with my degree. I want to focus on getting my diploma so I can move on with the rest of my life."

"Well, that's respectable, I guess." And Maggie didn't sound one bit like she meant it.

A sudden chill filled our usually warm dorm, and it wasn't because Gillian had set the air conditioning on maximum blast. My roommates only knew the side of me I'd shown them. They didn't know what to make of the other side of me, the one Juan also knew about, that girl who sounded older than her years and "too formal." Maggie and Gillian had been happy to accept me as a careless fool, and I guess I threw the balance off our equation.

After a while, I excused myself, explaining that I was tired from the trip. I went into my room to organize my thoughts. I couldn't ask Gillian to approach Juan at the Zoo for me and get his address. She'd start getting ideas, and it was obvious she'd object to my plans to win Juan over.

The good news was that I might not have to track down the Kensingtons to find the starting location of their fly-away mailbox. I could just... *What? Show up at the zoo and look for him?*

It sounded workable except for one huge thing. I really, really did not like zoos. When my dad had his breakdown and just vanished, I was alone in that odd place, and terrified. All the captive animals suddenly turned from curiosities to menaces. Every screech, growl and caw was unbearable to my ears. Even the helpful people at the zoo frightened me. I didn't know them. But then came the horror, when the police finally found my father wandering in circles through the forest on the other side of the creek at the western limit of the zoo. They took him away, bound and screaming. There was nothing I could do to make them set him free. All that time I could only count on the kindness of strangers, which thinned as the clock advanced its steady pace. I went from lost lamb to nuisance quickly. After that, I mistrusted kindness from anyone, knowing it wouldn't last. When the police took me away to drive me home, I thought they were arresting me too. I didn't know they hadn't arrested my father—only had him committed—until days later. Then, I didn't know what committed meant. When I finally got to visit Dad, I understood. Committed was just a different prison, in a different sort of zoo.

Still, I'd have to overcome my dread of zoos if I wanted to find Juan again. I felt I could. Besides, I didn't really have to go *inside* the zoo. I only had to wait near the staff parking lot.

Once my wicked plan came together in my head, I packed a bag to take with me to the car dealership in the morning. Then I went to sleep, and I dreamt dark and delicious dreams. Even after I woke up, I could still taste Juan on my tongue.

Chapter 14

Note for the future: Juan doesn't enjoy being tailed.

THOUGH I LEFT EARLY for the car dealership, booking an Uber before Maggie and Gillian were up, I still didn't get all the way South to the Zoo until well after lunch. While the Turnpike had been cleared, traffic everywhere was just awful. Most of Miami had re-located somewhere north and the usual traffic patterns were off with everyone who had to work driving south to get there. Traffic was never good in Dade County, but now it was bumper to bumper for endless miles. I could see from the highway that the destruction had been pretty bad, worse than I could have imagined. Some-how, seeing the rubble cleared out—even part of the way—made the damage seem worse. Miami was barren and broken.

The heat was insufferable. Though my new Audi had fantastic air conditioning, there was only so much the car could do to fight the effects of the bright sun.

I had a full tank of gas when I set off, but with the air blasting and the slow progress, I was really burning up fuel. Mindful that it was still hard to get gas, and seeing evidence of that in the long lines at several gas stations I passed along the way, I accepted the heat and opened my windows. The South Florida humidity was now back with a vengeance, and I was boiling. I prayed for a summer afternoon thunder-shower, though that was uncharitable to those who were still living with temporary tarp roofs over their heads.

As a result, by the time I arrived at the Zoo, and found the staff parking lot behind the fence where Juan's green Jeep was parked, I had wilted. My carefully applied make-up was running and my curls had frizzed wherever they weren't drip-ping sweat. I took some time to fix that while I waited for Juan to come out. I could put my face back on, but there was nothing much I could do about my hair in this climate. There was a lot of time to kill, I figured, not knowing Juan's work schedule exactly. I picked up my phone and logged into the university to catch up on the classes I was missing. Maybe I should have gone back to class, instead of driving down to the Zoo to find a man who might not want to see me. But I really wanted to see him. I needed to know how he would react, and whether he would keep his word to make me stay. After Juan and I came to an understanding of what that meant, I could go back to my classes.

That was my plan, anyway.

I almost missed Juan driving out. I had my eyes glued to my phone screen watching a recorded lecture. When I glimpsed up, his Jeep was already backing out of the parking space. I rushed to restart my engine and get out of the larger main parking lot so I could follow behind him. Right off the bat, I was confused. I had expected him to head toward the Turnpike, but he took some back roads instead. They had cleared out most of the rubble, but some of the roads in

South Dade were barely roads to begin with. Juan wove through farmland. It was all taking much longer than I thought. I had the GPS display up on my car and it looked like we were heading south, but sometimes we'd go west and other times east, and we even went north again for a short while. That's when I got suspicious. Was Juan just taking a joy ride? Suddenly, though, we were at a small airport. Juan stopped right in the middle of the road. There was no one around for miles. I stopped my car and waited. This hadn't been exactly the sort of reunion I had imagined. I had hoped to follow him home, but he'd obviously figured out he was being tailed.

He put his angry face right through my open window and shouted, "Why *the fuck* are you following me?"

I just stared at him for a while.

"*Well?*" he barked.

"It's me."

"*Who?*"

"It's me. Jenny Banks."

It was his turn to stare. Juan's face went from anger to surprise to disgust. I guess I had done too good a job of putting on my face. He hadn't recognized it, and I could see from his expression that he didn't exactly approve of my fully made-up look, either. I'd just wanted to be sure that he saw me as I was—an attractive grown woman, not the mess of a girl he somehow thought me to be.

"What is in your silly little head, Jenny Banks? Do you know how dangerous it is to tail someone like me?"

"I didn't have a choice," I said. "You never gave me your phone or address."

"I sent you a *message* to leave me the fuck alone."

I suppose he meant through that useless detective, but I wasn't going to even acknowledge hiring him.

"Really? I didn't get it. I lost my phone during Hank,

remember? Though, I've got a new one. Do you want the number?"

"Go back to college, Jenny Banks."

"No."

"Excuse me?"

"You heard me, Juan Ruiz. I will not go back to college. Take me home."

"No."

"You promised."

"No, I didn't."

"Yes, you did."

"Jenny, I don't have time for this shit. I'm tired to the bone."

"So, take me home. I'll take good care of you."

"There is *no home*, Jenny Banks!"

"What do you mean?"

"Forget you ever met me, Jenny," he said. "I'm dead, as far as you're concerned."

"No, Juan, that will not work for me. Sorry."

"Jesus, woman. Get a clue. Go away!"

"Nope."

Juan shook his head and then stormed off, heading back to his Jeep. I worried for a minute that he'd come back with a gun, or shoot me right from his Jeep with his rifle. He didn't, though. He just started his engine and turned around. I followed right behind him, even as he sped up and took wild turns around the perimeter of the farms, until I completely lost track of which direction we were headed. He was the direction. No matter where he went, I followed. When he got on the Turnpike, driving like a madman, weaving in and out of lanes, I followed. When he left Dade County far behind and headed further south to the Keys, I kept up. When he crossed seven mile bridge like he had a death wish, I was grateful for the turbo power of my car's engine. I didn't lose

Juan until we got all the way to Key West. Unfortunately, though, traffic proved to be a problem. I could not run the same red light as he did. He turned off and vanished into the charming grid of wood houses and street shops.

I cursed him for a while, but then my anger settled. I tried to imagine where I would go if I was Juan. Probably not Sloppy Joes, tempting as that sounded at that moment.

Then I remembered he said his cousins had got into his house because he'd been out fishing in Key Largo. People fished in Key West too, right? I set off for the marina. Well, all the marinas, one by one. I let my GPS lead the way, and looked for that Jeep. When I didn't find it anywhere on Key West, I headed back North on a hunch that Juan had just been fucking with me.

Now, I know at this point I sound pathetic chasing after a man all the way to the tail end of Florida and back. That's because I *was* pathetic. My only justification is that I was desperately in want of Juan. No, it was more than that. Juan had set me a challenge, and I thought I'd met it. I needed him to agree I'd done it. I needed him to tell me he recognized I'd changed my party girl ways because he'd asked. Then, if he said he'd backed out of his side of the deal completely, it was down to him. He was the asshole. I'd straightened myself out and I would move on with my life. I just needed to hear him *say* it.

It would have been nice to have another wild session with Juan before we parted ways forever, but I'd be happy with him just saying, "Jenny Banks, you are not the mess of a girl I pre-judged you to be. You are stronger than I thought. You are a good girl who just likes to be bad sometimes."

Or something like that, anyway.

Yeah, I was pathetic. Don't think I didn't know it either. As I kept driving from marina to marina all the way past Stock Island and Boca Chica and back over seven mile bridge, I told myself I would never find Juan this way and I should just get back to college, focus on my life, and forget the man forever.

Of course, I could just go to the zoo every day until he tired of having me chase him. But no, I knew if I hadn't succeeded tonight, I was better off letting him go. He was just a fucking guy, after all. *Didn't I have any self-respect left? Was I so fucking needy?* The strange thing was I could hear *him* asking *me* those questions, and it only made me angry again. I no longer knew whether I was angry with him or with myself. Mostly with myself, I guess.

Tired, thirsty, hungry, and needing to pee, I stopped at a Tiki bar on the water somewhere before Key Largo. It was a nice little place where I could just enjoy the sunset and the cool breeze. I wasn't looking for Juan anymore. I just wanted a bathroom, some seafood, and maybe a margarita. I figured, I'd earned one or six. The friendly blonde bartender gave me a warm, generous smile and offered some sympathy.

"What will you have, hon?" she asked. "You look like you're having a bad day. How about a nice cold beer?"

God, I wanted to say yes. Just sure. Beer. Beer would be good. Great, even.

"Can I just have a glass of water, for now, and the menu?"

"Of course!" She was very perky as she filled a large tumbler with ice chips and water, and handed over a little turquoise menu card with a crab emblem on it.

"Oh, you have stone crabs?"

"Yep, super fresh from the fish market next door. Everything here is the day's catch. Well, except for the smoked fish dip, because that's smoked, but it's delicious too."

"Okay, I guess I'll have three stone crab claws, to start."

"Anything with that?"

"A margarita?" I hesitated. "No, actually. Well, could I have a virgin one?"

"So, like, lemonade? Just the mix and ice? Or do you want the salt and lime too?"

"She doesn't want lemonade, Luanne," a deep voice said behind me. "Give her the tequila."

Luanne gave the voice a hard look, smirked, then rolled her eyes and shrugged.

I felt ready to pop, but I refused to turn around. "I'll just have the lemonade. No salt. I'll take the lime," I told Luanne.

"Sure, hon." She winked at me and got busy making my drink at the other end of the bar. I had the sense she was just trying to get away from the menace behind me. Though they knew each other. Or maybe not. Luanne had her name emblazoned on the crab pinned on her baby blue V-neck t-shirt, just to the right of her cleavage.

I sipped my water like I was completely alone, like I couldn't feel his heat cutting off the breeze, which had been so gently stroking my back.

"How the fuck did you find me, Jenny Banks?" he whispered in my ear.

I refused to answer him. He was an annoying ghost who would disappear again at any moment. I'd already decided I was better off not being haunted by him. Hadn't I? I thought I had just five minutes earlier. It wasn't easy, though, because my pussy fluttered with excitement and my core was already dripping. *Damn him.*

"Well?" he asked, again, sitting on the bar stool to my right.

"I stopped looking," I said.

"What does that mean?"

"I just came here. I wasn't looking for you. Why are you here, anyway? Have you been tailing me?"

The possibility had just occurred to me he'd only disoriented me, thinking I was chasing him. I hadn't seen him in my rear-view mirror, but I was mainly focused forward. Besides, he was far better at tailing people than I was.

"Why would I do that?"

"Why do you do anything, Juan Ruiz?"

"Some days, I'm not sure," he said. "But today I am."

"Yeah?" I asked, still trying not to look at him. It was really hard though. I couldn't miss his powerful hands grasped in front of him on the polished wood of the bar, trying to squeeze the life out of each other.

"Yeah."

I waited for him to elaborate, but he didn't. Luanne returned with my lemonade just then and asked Juan what he wanted to drink. "I'll have a beer," he said. *Asshole.* "Just whatever you have on tap. Nothing fancy."

"Did you want anything to eat?" Luanne asked.

"Stone crabs. Six claws."

Luanne smiled and winked at him, but not in a way that made me feel too jealous. She was just a perky, friendly woman. "You got it." Then Luanne set off to pour Juan's beer, only coming back to place it on the same Islamorada Brewing Company coaster she'd given me for my lemonade.

"Is this *still* Islamorada?" I asked her, confused. I thought I'd passed that key before stopping.

"No, they just supply, but you *are* close," Luanne explained. "You're at the Mar Bar in Tavernier, hon."

"Best little spot in the keys, if you ask me," Juan said. I hadn't asked him, though, and didn't like how his suddenly sweet comment brought out Luanne's charming dimples. The bartender thanked him and walked away to take care of another couple who had just sat on the other end of the bar. Well, *they* were a couple. Juan and I were just two people.

"So, is this your regular watering hole?" I asked when I couldn't take the silence anymore.

"Never been here before."

"So why *are* you here, then?" I turned to face him, wishing I could wipe that smirk off his face.

"Why'd you go to the zoo?"

"Because you promised me something."

He nodded. "There you go."

What the hell did that mean?

He took a long drink of his beer, practically draining the large plastic cup.

"I don't like the makeup," he said, right out of the blue. "You don't need it."

"Well, when I don't wear it, I look too young."

"You look fresh and real, and beautiful," he told the mostly empty cup he was hugging with both hands.

"And too young," I repeated.

He turned to face me, cupping my face and caressing my cheek gently with his thumb as his fingers stroked my earlobe. "Maybe not." Then Juan leaned in close, drawing me to him, until we were both practically falling out of our bar chairs into each other, and he gave me a soft kiss on the lips. "Fine, baby. Have it your way. Let's go home."

"What about our stone crabs?"

He got out of his chair and put a fifty-dollar bill on the bar counter, more than enough to cover both our orders. "We'll take them to go."

"To go where, exactly?" I stayed in my chair. "You said there was no home earlier. Did something happen to your house?"

"We have another place to go. I think you'll like it better."

I didn't like that he avoided my question, but I figured he had his reasons. "Okay."

"Good girl."

"I'm not, really."

"I'll tell you when you're bad, Jenny Banks. You never have to worry about that."

I smiled, threw my arms over his shoulders and jumped off the bar stool to wrap myself around his hot torso. Juan's swift reflexes claimed my rear, holding me up as he gave me the sort of kiss I really needed. Our tongues were all 'welcome back, I missed you, I never thought I'd see you again, and I thought I'd die.' Then they advanced to 'I'm gonna fuck you until you forget your name.' A few bar patrons hooted and whistled.

Luanne came back, saw Juan's money on the bar and figured out we wanted to take our crabs to go without our having to say it.

I still didn't know where we were going, and I honestly didn't care.

Chapter 15

We didn't get very far, but we went all the way.

I NEVER MADE it to my car. Juan took me by the hand and walked me over to his Jeep. When I argued I couldn't leave my new car behind, he said it would be safe where I'd parked it, and assured me we'd be back to pick it up in the morning. "I don't want you getting lost."

"I won't get lost if you're not rushing off to lose me."

Juan gripped my chin and gave me a stern look. "Where we're going, your car won't make it. Trust me, Jenny Banks. Get in."

I stuck my tongue out at him. "You're so bossy."

"Feel like getting in trouble right away, little one?"

"If possible, yes."

Juan smirked, opened the door to the jeep for me to get inside, and smacked my ass hard as I turned to step in. It was a good start to the evening, I thought.

We turned out of Mar Bar to head back south, which I

found confusing. I hoped we weren't going back all the way to Key West, because I really couldn't take crossing seven mile bridge a third time in one day. It made me nervous to be on a narrow highway so high over all that water.

"So you've been living in the Keys?"

"For a while."

"Long commute to the zoo, though. Isn't it?"

"Not really," he said. "It's working out well for me. I'm driving in the opposite direction of traffic. Except for the mobile homes, the Keys came through Hank better off than our part of Dade. Plus, this way I have my boat."

"You have your boat where we're going?"

"Yes, it's on the water."

"Nice."

"Do you like fishing, little one?"

"I've never done it before. I do *like* fish. Well, except tuna with mustard."

Juan chuckled. "You're never going to let me live that down, are you?"

"No. It's the best proof I have that you're not always right."

"I *was* right. It was nourishment."

"So are grasshoppers, and I'm not having any of those, either."

We went over a shorter bridge back to Islamorada and then Juan turned off onto a gravel road surrounded by mangroves. He was right. My car might have had some trouble navigating all the potholes. I was bouncing in the seat as it was. Then we turned left onto a road which was not in much better condition, and arrived at an old, white, wood, hurricane house on stilts. Juan parked underneath the house by the large utility room built around the center pile. When I got out, I saw a pool in the gravel lined backyard, and a canal behind the house where a large fishing boat was moored.

"I thought you said you went fishing in Key Largo."

"Yeah, the place where I used to stay in Key Largo is gone," Juan said. "It was older than this place, and not as sturdy. I rented this place for the time being. I'm thinking of keeping it, though."

"Yeah?" I followed him up the front stairs to the screened-in porch at the entrance to the house. "What about your old house?"

"I don't want to talk about that right now," Juan said, opening the screen door.

The screened porch wrapped around the house, offering plenty of places to sit, enjoy the breeze and look out on the canals and the ocean beyond them. Juan opened the front door, white with a large oval frosted and carved glass inset to let in more light, and I followed him into a bright white living room, which led to a small dining area and well-equipped kitchen with an open bar.

They decorated everything in white with some turquoise and navy decor, including a long navy sign over the large windows in the dining area which read: 'Fish, Eat, Sleep, Repeat.' There was a blue marlin trophy hanging above the larger sofa against the wall, opposite a flat-screen television, and double-sliding glass doors beyond that which led out to the back of the screened-in porch.

"This is very nice," I said, wrapping my arms around myself, "and cold."

"The central air conditioner here works really well," he said, coming to wrap his arms around me after putting our crab legs in the fridge. "Are you chilly, baby? I can make you warm."

"Yes, please. I'm freezing."

Juan kissed the top of my head. "Let's go to bed, Jenny Banks."

"I wish you wouldn't call me by my full name," I grumbled as he led me down the hall, still wrapped in his arms, to the large master bedroom.

"I'll call you whatever I like, Jenny. You're mine now. Remember?"

"Am I?"

"Yes." He lifted me up in his arms, carrying me like a baby the rest of the way. "You're my naughty, disobedient, little slut."

I giggled until he tossed me on the bed so hard I bounced on the large mattress. Juan ordered me to strip and started to undress himself. After kicking off my tan moccasins, I took my time unbuttoning my jeans and shimmying out of them inch by inch. Juan's gaze burned me all the while, as he pulled off his shirt, revealing that hard chest I'd grown so fond of, and the defined six-pack below. When he reached for the buckle of his belt, my breath hitched.

"Jenny, if you don't hurry and get naked, I'm going to whip you," he said. "Or is that what you want, little one?"

"Well, you know," I said, with a pout, "just however much you think I earned."

"You chased me all the way to Key West," he said, "and wasted a lot of gas. I'd say you earned enough of a whipping to be real sore for the rest of the week."

"Okay."

"But I want to fuck your ass. So take off all your clothes, turn around on the mattress and lie on your belly. Now, Jenny Banks. Do it."

"Yes, sir."

I rushed to comply, tossing my jeans and my t-shirt over the side of the bed, and then throwing my bra at Juan before pulling off my panties and tossing those at him, too. I spread my legs for him, briefly, giving him a good luck at my glistening pussy, before I finally turned over on my belly. I bent my legs up, kicking my feet at him, then crossed my ankles. Juan went over to the nightstand on the left and pulled out a large tube of lube.

"Have you been having a lot of fun without me, Juan Ruiz? Or were you expecting me?"

"A soldier is always prepared, Jenny Banks," he said, coming back to the end of the bed to pull my legs apart and kneel behind me on the mattress. "Part those full cheeks for me, slut, and beg me to teach you a lesson."

"Are you saying my ass is big?" I asked, teasing.

"Just right-sized," he said, pulling me by the hips so I was on my knees, with my top resting on the mattress. "Open it up for me now, baby."

It was embarrassing, which I know was what he wanted, but also thrilling. I reached back to part my butt-cheeks, exposing my pucker to him, and Juan dripped a long stream of lubricant down my crack. Then he put down the tube and worked the lube into my sphincter with his thick index finger. The penetration and the anticipation of more made my whole pussy tingle pleasantly, but I knew his oversized cock would feel different.

"Beg, Jenny Banks."

"Please," I said. "Can you teach me a lesson?"

"Why?" he asked, still working his finger slowly in and out of my narrow entrance.

"Because I came back when you warned me to stay away."

"What kind of lesson do you think you deserve, then?"

"A hard lesson in being owned, sir."

Juan began stroking my pussy with the thick head of his cock.

"I agree, Jenny. You deserve a very hard lesson in being owned."

When he pulled his finger away. I was ready for him to replace it with his cock, but nowhere near as roughly as he did. One hard thrust and he filled me completely, I felt his balls slap against my pussy. I cried out as he gripped my ass with both hands and kept pumping harder. I strained to take all of him this way, grasping the light blue quilted bedspread, tears filling my eyes.

"I warned you," he said between jagged breaths. "Serving your master... Will hurt."

"Yes."

"But you enjoy the pain?"

"Yes."

"You want more?"

"Yes."

"How much?"

"All of it."

I wanted Juan to use me every way he had threatened to back in his old house. I needed to be his rag doll. Already the pain I felt had transformed into something building up from my core to coat my body in tingling heat from the inside out. I was sweating, despite the cold air blowing into the room. Juan bent over me to cover my body, his heat blending with mine as his thrusts quickened, and he released himself inside of me.

"Rag doll," he said, grunting. "You'll come to regret it."

I smiled as he collapsed beside me and I turned to curl up against him, dragging my fingernail over the damp channel of his chest up to his muscular neck, stroking his Adam's apple, and then up under his chin to tap the dimple. "I won't."

Juan rose on his elbow, pushing me on my back. "Spread

those legs wide for me and play with your clit. Make yourself come."

"You could help," I suggested.

He sat up, spreading my legs wide with a rough tug, and bringing my hand to my pussy. "Stroke yourself, baby. I want to see you do it."

I dragged my fingers along the length of my vulva, gathering all the moisture and reawakening my sensitive flesh. I reached the nub as he wanted, stroking, flicking and tugging while Juan watched. My breathing became erratic and my body quivered as I neared the edge. Juan pressed my legs open, thrusting two fingers deep into my channel to stroke the tender spot that set me ablaze. I gasped. "Look at me, Jenny Banks," he commanded, pumping his fingers in and out. "Keep your eyes on me and your fingers on that little pearl." My eyes locked with his, the intensity of his gaze added to the heat building in my body. "From now on, you only come when I allow it. Understand?"

I could only nod. I could barely breathe, much less speak.

"Do you need to come, Jenny?"

I blinked slowly and nodded again.

With a wicked grin, he grabbed my wrist and drew my hand away from my clit. He pulled his fingers out of me at the same time and pinned both my wrists above my head. He hovered over my body, his lower torso pressed against my mons, teasing my needy pussy.

"Bad girls don't get to come," he said, his forehead resting against mine. "And you've been a very bad girl, Jenny."

"Aww," I complained, pouting. "You set me up. I had to find you again."

"No more showing up to my work uninvited or following me around Florida. Tailing me is a dangerous game."

"You promised you wouldn't let me go again if I showed up."

"I won't. You're my plaything now, so you have to do as you're told."

"I can do that."

"We'll see." Juan bit my lip and licked it, then kissed me roughly, forcing me to submit to the demands of his tongue. It made me ache to be filled. My core was hard as a knot. I tried to urge him by pushing my hips up against him, but he pulled back and jumped off the bed, dressing again. "Our crab legs are getting cold."

"They are supposed to be cold!"

"I'm hungry, Jenny, and you're being punished. Come to the dining room. We have to talk, anyway."

I groaned and rolled off the bed slowly, then searched for my scattered clothes, trying to find my panties.

"What are you doing?" Juan asked.

"Well, if we're going to eat…"

"Did I say you could dress?"

"You want me to eat naked?"

"You will be naked unless I tell you to dress," Juan said. "You will only ever wear clothes I approve of, and you will not wear that much make-up anymore. Now, go to the bathroom and wash up. When you're done, meet me in the dining room."

"What if somebody comes over?"

"Nobody comes here, Jenny. I'm not a very sociable guy, if you haven't noticed."

"Except with Luanne."

"Jealous?"

"A little."

"Good."

I took a while in the bathroom because I decided I needed a shower if I was going to go around naked. Juan still didn't have any decent products for my hair and unfortunately, my things were in my car. I hoped this one would still be where I parked it the next day. I couldn't afford to keep buying new cars every time we got together.

When I finally got to the living room, Juan had switched off the air conditioning and opened the sliding glass doors. That was fortunate because I would have frozen sitting in the dining room naked. The evening was warm, though there was a sea breeze. The night would be warm too, in the middle of summer. But there was enough chill remaining in the house to be comfortable.

Juan had already set our crabs on plates and put a beer on the table mat by my seat, which was catty corner, to his right, at the head of the table.

"I thought you didn't want me drinking anymore."

"I never want you getting drunk again. If I ever catch you drunk, I'm going to skin your backside. That doesn't mean you can't enjoy a drink with me. Only with me, Jenny Banks."

I sat next to him on the white wood chair of the dining room set and clinked beer bottles with him before taking a long, grateful swig of Sol. It was light, and delicious. "Do you have to keep calling me that? You just do it to annoy me now."

He smiled at that. "You do plenty to annoy *me*. I figure we're even. Like I said, I will call you whatever I want to call you, pet."

"Suit yourself, Juan Ruiz."

He reached over and took the beer bottle out of my hand just as I was about to take a second swig. "You will call me, sir. You will be respectful or you will get no treats."

"Sorry, sir," I said meekly, but I didn't get my beer back.

"So tell me what a good girl you were all this time that you spent in Pennsylvania." He cracked open one of the crab claws, dipping it in the mustard mayonnaise the restaurant had given us and brought the white flesh to my mouth. I took a bite and savored its sweet and tangy freshness.

"Nothing to tell," I said as soon as I'd swallowed. "I did what you asked."

"I didn't ask you to do anything," Juan cracked a crab for himself.

"Yes, you did. You said I shouldn't drink and I shouldn't be with any other guys, so I did that."

"You weren't with any other guys, huh?" Juan fed me another bit of crab claw.

"Nope. Don't want them. How about you? Were you with any other women?"

"Dozens," he said. "I had all this free time on my hands."

"Seriously?"

"Of course."

"No, you didn't. You were waiting for me to come back."

"Nope. I never wanted you back, remember? In fact, I sent a simple message that you should stay away, which you ignored." Juan stuffed his mouth with more crab, but there was a small dimple in his cheek and a glint in his eye which reassured me he was full of shit.

"But you won't have time for other women now, right?"

Juan thought about that while he cracked another crab claw to stuff its meat into my mouth.

"Well, considering how much trouble you can get yourself into, I guess I'll be too busy for other bitches."

I swallowed the big bite of crab he fed me. "Good."

"Are you a very jealous woman, slut?"

"Terribly, horribly jealous. I don't like to share *at all*."

"Since when?"

"Since the helicopter ride."

Juan laughed a boisterous laugh, which interrupted his crab claw cracking. I reached for one to crack myself, and he gently tapped my hand away. Okay, message received. Feeding me was his job now. I could live with that. He took the crab claw and broke the hard shell. "What was it about riding in a helicopter that turned you into a jealous wench?"

"Well, you got out, kissed me, and then you went away. You didn't even look back."

"And that made you jealous?"

"That made me think I might never see you again, which made me angry and frustrated. I never want to feel that way again. So the prospect that you might find someone else to play with makes me jealous."

"You're not going sweet on me, Jenny Banks. I've told you I suck at relationships."

"No, I only want you for sex, but I don't want anyone else to have you."

Juan nodded. "Okay, we'll see how long you feel that way. I give it a couple of days, at most, before you decide I'm too much for you."

"Say you're glad I'm back. Admit it."

Juan stuffed my mouth with more crab.

"Jenny, do you think you'd be sitting here in my dining room naked, eating crab, if I didn't want you to be here? But I'm only using your round, soft, luscious body. You're here because of those two bountiful tits and that luscious balloon of an ass. Do you understand?"

It flattered me, to be honest. It's always nice to be appreciated, although it was hardly the first time I heard a man tell me I was desirable.

"Well, I'm only using you for that freaky dick of yours, and all that muscle you've got helps." I winked at him, then added, "And that *scalding hot* mean streak of yours. It all suits me fine."

Juan smiled and ate some crab out of the bits of shell that still had meat in them. He was an expert at picking through the bones. Then he cracked another claw for me.

"You can do better than me. By the time I'm done with you, you'll know that for a fact."

"I haven't found better yet, and I've been looking for a while."

Juan let that thought settle in his head as he sipped his beer. Then he passed me the bottle he'd taken away earlier.

"How's your family doing?"

I shrugged, drank more of my beer, and told him everything that had happened. It was weird saying any of it out loud. I never discussed that part of my life with anyone, especially not my father's problems. I felt comfortable telling Juan because I felt he would understand. Besides, he'd seen the ugliness in me already, and he seemed to like me well enough, despite all that, to take me back. That's why I'd *really* chased Juan down and around the Keys. It wasn't because I needed to prove him wrong about me. He wasn't wrong. Not completely, anyway. I needed to be with someone who could see all of me—messed up as I was—and still want me. Juan hadn't let me down.

"Do you feel light now, little one?" he asked. My eyes stung he would remember what I'd told him during the hurricane. I blinked back the tears, swallowed the lump in my throat, and smiled at him.

"Yes, I feel light as a breeze."

"Good."

"How about you, Juan? Did you kill all the bad people who needed to die?"

"I'm still alive."

"Well, I'm very glad about that. Do you want to tell me what happened to the house?"

"No."

"Please? I told you my ugly thing. It's only fair."

He looked at me a while, then he cracked the last two crabs claws, fed one to me and took another for himself.

"There's nothing to tell, little one. Only nothing."

"But the house was mostly okay, right? I mean, yes, it was a mess, but you had the tarp on the roof…"

"It wasn't enough, Jenny. There were rains and heavy winds after we left. The tarp was only a temporary fix. I needed to have covered the roof with plywood, at least. But I didn't have time to do that. Then the looters finally got through. I came back to a broken, empty shell. Everything is gone."

"They took everything?"

"Except for a few things that I kept in my safe. They didn't crack that and they couldn't lift it. Fortunately, I had my weapons in there. They're here now, or on the boat. But they took all the furniture and appliances and a bunch of other irreplaceable things."

"Didn't they leave you anything?" I wondered about the album, to be honest. It had seemed so important to him, and had made it through two hurricanes. It would have been pointless and cruel for someone to take that.

Juan seemed to read my mind. "My memories are still intact, and I have my photos, thanks to you. But the house is a wreck. I'm not sure I'm up to rebuilding it again, to be honest. Life is loss and disappointment, Jenny. I don't really have to tell you that. I think you understand that better than most."

I nodded, and we sat in silence for a while, until I got the courage to ask a question I had avoided before. "Is your mother still alive?"

"No, she died a couple of years ago. Cancer."

"I'm sorry."

"Me too. She was the last good person I knew."

"What about your cousins and your uncle?"

"I told you before, they're very different people. We don't really get along. They've got money, and it's all they care about. My uncle helped us, after dad died, but it came with strings attached. My mother loved her brother, despite everything, because she was loyal and he was family. That means less to me than it meant to her. If they were ever in real trouble, I suppose I'd lend a hand. But mostly I try not to have anything to do with them if I can help it."

"You're heavy now, aren't you?" I asked, getting out of my chair to come sit on his lap. He made room for me and smiled as I put my arms over his shoulders.

"Not as heavy as I was this morning." Juan drew me into a tender kiss that blossomed into something warmer, reawakening the desperate need I'd felt earlier.

"Jenny, if we're going to do this, you need to do everything I say. Do you understand?"

"Yes, sir."

"If you change your mind at any point, just tell me it's over and go. But once you do that, there will be no coming back."

"I won't change my mind."

"It won't be easy."

"I don't want easy. I want you."

Juan kissed me again, this time demanding more of me. I felt warm, pressed against him, and so very light. My only discomfort was the stinging of my hard nipples and the pinching and heat in my ravenous core.

"Do you think you're going to let me come soon?"

"Baby, I'm going to make you come until you beg me to stop."

"That could take a while."

Juan lifted me in his arms and carried me back to the bedroom. "Let's get started, then."

Chapter 16

So much coming and so many tears. And so much coming.

JUAN TORE the bed open with one hand, laying me down on the soft white cotton sheet that covered the mattress and pulling a couple of pillows from the other side of the bed to place under my ass. He went to the dresser, pulled out a set of leather cuffs lined with soft sheepskin, which he looped through one of the iron bars at the headboard, and bound my wrists over my head. Then he left.

"Where are you going?" I called after him.

"Shower. Relax. I'll be quick."

It was hard to relax, exposed as I was, aching for him, but I tried my best. I thought about my situation, whether I was doing the right thing by giving Juan so much control over me, but all I felt was light. And safe. It took very little time for him to come out of the bathroom, naked and gorgeous, little beads of water glistening gold on his tan skin in the warm amber light of sunset. We missed that, but there would be plenty of time to see the sunset another day. Just then, all I could see was Juan rise, his cock hardening to a wide, menacing weapon as he approached me again on the mattress. He knelt at the foot of the bed without saying a word, his eyes tracing the curves of my body. Then he parted my legs slowly, gently, caressing my inner thighs, kissing my right knee. Juan came closer to kiss the fullness of my inner thigh just south of the crease of my pussy. He skipped past that quivering, wet, tender place that so needed his attention and kissed the inside of my other thigh instead.

He rose to lick my lower belly with his hard, pointy tongue, from just above my mons to my belly button, and then he dipped the tip of his tongue in there, swirling it around, sending an electric rush running through me and a hard pull in my womb. I drew in a sharp breath and wiggled my hips, but Juan would not be rushed. He trailed that tongue through the channel of my torso and when he reached my breasts he lifted and licked the crease underneath, then circled them to lick my areola, which only made my nipples swell to bursting. He ignored those needy tips, and licked my chest, lathering the dip in my clavicle with his tongue before working his way to the heated pulse of my neck and sucking me like a vampire, marking me with his teeth. After he left his mark, he moved up to my earlobe, biting that hard before whispering, "You're my pretty pet now, Jenny. Aren't you? Only mine."

"Yes," I breathed in response.

"I am going to make you regret the day you met me, little one. I am going to make you plead to me to let you go."

He took my breath away with an invasive kiss, starting with a peck at my jaw before claiming my lips like he wanted to bruise them. I let his magical tongue in and caressed it with my own, welcoming his intrusion and his demands, greeting him as my master, promising him my full submission.

Juan accepted my acquiescence and bit my lower lip, before working his way back down, biting one of my nipples as he squeezed the other hard. I squeaked with pleasure. He bit the side of one hip as he pinched the other, eliciting a gasp. I raised my hips to him again, urging him to focus on where he was most wanted, but Juan would not be rushed. He kissed my belly again, and nibbled on my bare mons, then poked the cleft in my labia with his tongue, briefly stroking my clit, and then sat up on his heels.

When I whimpered, Juan gave me a grin that was all teeth and menace, his eyes dark and burning with desire. He couldn't deny it—that cock of his upright like a staff, dark pink and dangerous. Then he turned around on the bed, straddling me so that his head lay between my legs, and his engorged cock hovered over my head, within reach of my lips.

"Suck, baby girl," he commanded before parting my labia to feast on my folds. I licked the glistening head and licked the seam and the stem before wrapping my lips around it and sucking it deeper into my mouth. He moaned for me, his mouth hot against my lower lips. Each time I suckled as he pushed deeper into my mouth, his tongue rewarded my clit. He thrust his fingers into me as he nibbled on my nub and I hummed against his cock head as his hips urged me to take him deeper still. Soon, we were both ready to burst. He came first, filling my throat with his warm seed, and I came for him after he bit my sensitive nub.

Except he wasn't done with me. Juan continued to pump his fingers into me, stroking my G-spot as his tongue and his lips revered my clit and soon I was panting for him again. When I lifted my head to his cock, licking the tender tip, he flinched and dismounted from me. "I'll come again for you soon enough. For now, I want you crying, little one." Sitting at the end of the bed again, he parted my lower lips with one hand, and gave my clit the full attention of his mouth until my panting intensified and I gripped the bar which held my cuffs in place. He brought his tongue lower and penetrated me with the flexible muscle, as one of his fingers flicked at my clit. My hips bucked as a second orgasm overtook me and I came on his tongue. He licked me whole, then rose above me, hard and huge again. Juan brought his cock to my entrance and penetrated me with a sudden deep thrust that slammed my cervix. I cried out, both in pain and pleasure as he pounded into me, resting one arm on my pillow and stroking my bound wrists, while his free hand gripped my throat. "Does it hurt enough, baby?" he asked between ragged breaths. "Is your Master's cock punishing you right?"

Tears filled my eyes, but it wasn't from pain alone. It was from the fierce beauty of this moment as his powerful body overwhelmed my senses. All the nerves in my body ignited, pricking like pop-rocks inside and out.

"Answer me, slut," Juan commanded, his hips doubling the order with a hard knock on the limit of my sheath.

"Yes," I said, barely able to get the word out.

"Yes *what?*" Juan asked, the 'what' accompanied by another pummeling from his brutish member. He was going to tear me open and I wanted him to. I had needed this ache. I had longed for it for years and never imagined I would ever get it.

"Yes, Master." I wept.

"Come again for me," he said, his thrusts quickening as he let himself loose, the pounding on my cervix intensifying. A knot built up and pinched where he struck as my walls convulsed around him, gripping the full girth of him, tightening, making each penetration more intense. Juan pushed through my walls each time. The abundant juices I produced aided his rough invasion, but I knew as an unholy groan escaped my lips that I would still be sore in the morning. Juan released my neck to grip my left thigh and lifted my leg as he pressed himself deep to eject his seed inside me. With me pinned on his cock, the aftermaths of my orgasm continuing, Juan released my leg, slapped my left breast with a grin, gripped my chin, and descended on my mouth, crushing my lips, as his tongue rewarded me for my suffering.

"*Un coño de seda*," he sighed.

"What does that mean?" I asked.

"You've got a deliciously adaptable little cunt, do you know that?" he asked. "I love being inside of you."

"Do you like my cunt better than my ass?"

He thought about that for a moment. "It's different. Your ass yields to me and sucks me in real nice, but your hungry little pussy fights back, gripping my dick. It also stretches really well, allowing all of me inside. Not every woman can take what I've got. Like I told you, whenever you deserve a punishment, I will fuck your ass hard. I may not always be as generous with lube as I was today. When you've been good, I'll fuck your pussy hard."

"Okay," I said, smiling at him. "That sounds fair."

"Speaking of fair, it's time for you to pay for chasing me to the Keys," Juan said, stroking my lips with his thumb.

"I thought that was what the ass fucking was punishment for—wasn't it?"

"That was part of it, yes. But I fucked you in the ass to please myself. Now it's time to give you what you wanted."

"What do you mean?"

"You know what I mean, Jenny. What did you ask for?"

"No, I mean… I wasn't asking for you to whip me. I only thought that you might."

"I will. I want to see you crying and begging me to let you go, remember?"

"I will not ask you to let me go, Juan. No matter what you do, I won't just go away. And you can't make me. You promised."

"We'll see how long you feel that way." Juan pulled out of me then raising himself on the bed to flip me over so I faced my bound wrists, my torso resting on the mattress as he pulled my hips up to place me on my knees, my ass up in the air.

I still remembered his previous spankings, so I was braced for some considerable pain, but memory is an unreliable measure. The moment his hand contacted my rear, my body rebelled, my ass clamped with pain, and I was flat on the bed again. "Oh, no, Jenny, you will stay in position," Juan said, lifting my hips. "The more you move, the more you get." Juan smacked my rear again. This time, the other butt cheek, and I struggled to stay in position as the searing heat of his hand moved up my spine. I did pretty well for a while longer as he switched between one cheek and the other. By well, I only mean that I kept my ass up. I was wailing by the tenth hard smack, tears falling liberally from my eyes. I pleaded with him to stop. Of course, he didn't, not until my entire rear was ablaze—the fullness of my cheeks, the crevice where the curve of my butt met my upper thighs, and the upper thighs themselves. Then he parted my legs wider and smacked my pussy. That was it for me. My pussy was already sensitive from his plowing, and his hand stung like hellfire. I howled.

But to my never-ending shame, my core tightened and my hunger increased. I wanted him again. So I begged him to fuck me.

"I won't be gentle," he warned. "You understand that, right?"

"Yes," I sobbed. "Please."

Juan mounted me, just as I was, perfectly presented to

him. He speared me with that rod, smacking his pelvis against my blazing rear. The soreness and ache I'd felt when he fucked me on my back was nothing compared to this. His hands gripped my hips so I couldn't escape an inch of him. I would never have thought I could take all of Juan this way, but apparently my vagina needed something bigger than average to stretch it. I came like a nuclear bomb had gone off in my head. I felt so completely satisfied each time he rammed me, so happy and so... Not just light... High. The actual word was high. Being fucked silly by Juan was better than being drunk. It was a smoother ecstasy than Molly, even if Juan was every bit as dangerous as the drug. I didn't care. He wasn't a danger to me. To me, he was heaven.

We collapsed together on the bed. Juan unfastened my wrists and pulled me up against his hot, sweaty body, then kissed the top of my head.

We lay in silence for a while, catching our breath. I waited to settle back into my body. Part of me was still floating somewhere in the ceiling.

"You're very good at this, little one," he said, finally. "That's a problem."

"Why is it a problem?" I asked, collecting a drop of sweat from his chest with my fingertips.

"A man could get addicted to such a willing sub. I avoid enjoying anything I couldn't easily quit."

"You promised."

"I know, and I will keep my promise," he said, stroking my back. It was so soothing, being nestled in his powerful arms, that I nearly fell asleep. He woke me out of it with a question.

"Do you want some ice cream, precious?"

"What flavor?"

"Buttered Pecan."

"Oh, yes, that sounds delicious. I'm crazy about Buttered Pecan."

Juan laughed.

"What?" I asked. "It's *great* ice cream. My favorite used to be strawberry, but I got hooked on Buttered Pecan here in Miami."

"I know. It's the only thing I'm addicted to, honestly. Well, it *was* the only thing."

"You're not going sweet on me, are you, Juan?"

Juan kissed the tip of my nose. "Do you feel sweet?"

"I feel deliciously wrecked."

"Good. Let's soothe some of that ache. Want to watch your cartoons while I spoon feed you ice cream?"

"Can I wear clothes? I think I'll be too chilly eating ice cream naked."

"You'll be sitting with me. I'll keep you warm."

"Even so."

"Okay, I'll loan you a shirt, but no bottoms. I want to see that red ass glowing in the dark."

"Deal."

Chapter 17

Lies lead to unnecessary complications.

I WISH I could tell you that Juan and I lived happily ever after, from that point on. We nearly did. I went back to college the next day, and he went back to the zoo. We agreed to meet back at Mar Bar for dinner. Then went home and fucked each other silly, and we ate more ice cream and watched more Disney movies. It made up for everything I'd missed out on growing up. I enjoyed every moment for weeks until I felt secure for the first time in a long time.

I think Juan felt secure in us too, though it was hard to tell. The army had trained him to be on alert, to be ready for the worst to come at a drop of a hat. He was always a spring ready to bounce. One day in late August, as I was getting ready to start my new semester and signing up for the internship I needed to complete my degree, I got a text message from Juan. It said, simply: *42*.

I knew what it meant. Life, the universe, and everything

had just put an end to our peace. Juan, who was a huge fan of Douglas Adams and The Hitchhiker's Guide to the Galaxy, had told me it would be his code if they ever deployed him again, so I would know not to come down to the Keys.

I told myself not to worry. After all, Juan was an expert killer. He knew what he was doing. Telling yourself not to worry is not as effective as it should be, though. After two weeks, I was more than worried. I was inconsolable.

I tried my best to focus on my classes and my internship, to avoid imagining all the scenarios scrolling through my head of how Juan might die somewhere in a foreign land; his body never returned with no one to claim it. My roommates, who had stuck around in the same room with me for another semester, were completely unaware that Juan was the mystery man with whom I'd been sleeping for weeks. They tried to cheer me up in their own weird way.

"You really fell for this guy, didn't you?" Maggie teased as she passed me a cup of instant cocoa with mini marshmallow floating on the surface. She claimed it was medicine, guaranteed to wipe out the blues. "I thought you didn't do relationships."

I took the cup from her and sipped a bit. It was much too sugary and a little too hot. I placed it down on the coffee table to cool and sat back on the sofa with my chilly bare feet tucked under my rear. "Yeah, well, it's *not* a relationship like I've told you dozens of times before—only steady sex. Or it *was* steady, anyway."

"Well, if all you want is sex…"

"I'm not interested, Maggie," I said.

After her four-way—which was awkward, something she swore never to do again—Maggie had settled on none of the men. Instead, she had started dating Robert—a guy she met at a bar in Fort Lauderdale—who seemed nice from the couple of times I'd run into him at our dorm. He was a motorcycle mechanic and had several rugged MC friends who Maggie was sure were just right for me. I don't know why Maggie always wanted me to be dating someone like whoever she was dating. I guess it just helped to reassure her she wasn't making a terrible mistake on her own. Not that I thought Robert was a mistake. He seemed to get Maggie, and he made her happy.

But I knew dating anyone but Juan would do irreparable damage to our deal. Assuming Juan ever came back.

"All I'm saying is you have to get back on the horse, even if it's a different horse," Maggie said, blowing on her own cup of cocoa as she put her puffy pink slippers on the coffee table.

"I don't want to ride, Maggie."

"Hmm, this guy must have been something," Gillian noted, joining us in the living room with a large tumbler of iced tea.

"Yeah," I said. "He was… He *is*." I worried about using the past tense when referring to Juan, like it might jinx him, somehow, assuming he wasn't already in trouble. Or dead.

"So, call him and tell him you're sorry about whatever it is he's upset with you about," Gillian suggested.

"It's not like that," I said.

"Well, then forgive him for whatever he did that upset you," Gillian persisted.

"He's just gone," I said.

"What, like *missing*?" Maggie asked, perking up to hear the story behind that.

"He's out on assignment, and unreachable," I said.

"Oh, is he a journalist?" Gillian asked.

I figured that was as a good a cover for what Juan did as any. It would explain a lot without my having to give away a thing. "Yeah, something like that."

"So is he like on assignment in the Arctic or something?" Maggie teased.

"Something. I don't really know where, to be honest. He doesn't tell me."

"Well, call whatever publication or whatever channel he works for," Gillian suggested. "He has to check in with them to file his stories."

"No, that would make me sound desperate. Plus, I don't think they'll just tell a stranger where he went."

I picked up my mug and drank a bit of the too-sweet cocoa. It really wasn't helping, so I put it back. I definitely would *not* call the army to ask them what had happened to Juan. Who would you call about something like that, anyway? I wouldn't know where to start. And Juan would probably never forgive me if I did.

"Well, hon, if he's just going to be gone for weeks at a time without being traceable, then you could definitely have a back-up guy," Maggie said. "I mean, I don't imagine he's going without wherever *he* is."

"No, Maggie," I said. "If I ever did that, I would lose him for sure."

"I don't know. That sounds like a relationship to me," Maggie said.

"I guess it is, but it's only sex." I drank more of the cocoa. It was tasting better.

"Then why are you so upset?" Maggie was determined to keep pushing the issue. In fairness, I'd brought it on by being so damned sad. I don't know. I just didn't feel right in my skin. "You walk around moping, like someone broke your heart or something."

"It's wonderful sex."

"What's his name?" Gillian asked, which was a reasonable question. They'd never pushed for much information before, just accepting that I was gone for days having a good time. But I was prepared in case it ever came up. "John," I replied.

"John what?"

"John Payne."

"*Pain*?" Maggie laughed.

I spelled it out for her, though the homonym had inspired me when I came up with Juan's fake identity. Not that I was ashamed of my relationship with Juan, but I already knew Gillian hated him and I didn't want anyone to know what he really did for a living. It was better this way.

Gillian got up and disappeared into her room for a while, which was a little abrupt, but I figured she went to get something.

"Where'd you meet him?" Maggie asked.

"On my flight back from Pennsylvania. We were sitting together on the plane. We just hit it off."

When Gillian came back, she had her bamboo-covered laptop with her. She sat cross-legged on the armchair with her laptop resting between her legs and she clicked keys right away. "I'll find him for you."

"No, that's okay, Gillian. If he comes back, he comes back. If he doesn't, I'll get over him."

"Again, this doesn't sound like it's just sex," Maggie observed. I shot her a look. "I'm just saying! If you have feelings for this guy, there's nothing wrong with that."

"Neither one of us wants that. We agreed to be exclusive about sex, but that's more about health than anything else. I don't believe relationships ultimately work out well for anyone. All you do is make each other miserable until one of you cracks."

"Yeah, that all sounds really rational and mature and stuff," Maggie said. "Except it's complete bullshit. The minute you count on a man to be your only man, you've already given him the power to make you miserable. Case in point, *you* right now."

"Aren't you exclusive with Robert now?"

"Yes, but that's only because I love him, and he loves me. We're as deeply in love as we are in lust."

"How do you know?"

"Well, he's my first thought when I wake up in the morning and my last thought when I go to sleep. He makes me feel appreciated and cared for, and I feel I can trust him. I tell him things I rarely talk about and he gets it. He's sexy as sin, which helps, but honestly, I just feel right around him. My mom always said that's what love is, feeling right with a person. Like, we're missing a piece of ourselves and when we find 'the one' that piece isn't missing anymore. You feel whole."

I tried not to think too much about how similar that was to what I felt for Juan. I couldn't be in love with him, though. That was just too risky.

"Does Robert know you feel this way?" I asked Maggie.

"Yeah, and he's said he feels the same way about me." Maggie beamed. "We've been talking about taking it further. Don't be surprised if I move in with him permanently."

"So when's the wedding?" It was my turn to tease Maggie.

She sipped some cocoa before answering me. "He has to ask. I'm very traditional that way."

She was serious, I noticed. This was something she'd been considering for a while. I couldn't believe it. How could anyone know for certain that they wanted to spend the rest of their lives with someone? Couldn't they see ahead to everything going wrong and falling apart?

"How will he deal with your medical school stuff?"

"Robert stays busy with his shop so he doesn't need me to work and he doesn't need me to be a housewife or anything like that. He just enjoys having me around and I enjoy having him around. He understands I'll be tied up for a few years with med school and my residency and all that, but he's okay with it."

"Well, I'm happy for you," I said, meaning it, as I raised my cocoa mug in a toast to her. After all, love was her pleasant delusion, and I had no business interfering. People never want to hear a truth they'd rather not acknowledge. They feel more at ease with a comforting fiction.

"You'll find 'the one' someday," she assured me. "Or maybe you already have, and you just don't know it."

"Well, Jenny's 'maybe the one' doesn't exist," Gillian said, which made Maggie gasp. "At least as far as I can find. There are no articles attributed to him anywhere. I'm sorry, but I think your dude is a liar, Jenny."

"Is that so?" I said, sipping my cocoa. "Well, I guess it serves me right for trusting him."

"That's *it*?" It shocked Maggie that I took the news so well. "Aren't you furious?"

"Why? Because he lied to me about being a journalist?"

"Well, *yeah*, for one." Maggie was angry on my behalf. "If he lied about that, then you can't believe anything else he says. I'm telling you, let him go. Just write him off for lost. I'll find you a guy you can trust."

"No, thanks, Maggie," I said. "I know you mean well, but I'm really not interested."

"So you *do* love this guy, even though he's a liar and probably a cheat, and definitely not a journalist."

"Can we talk about something else, please?" I begged. "Tell me more about Robert."

That took some pressure off, at least for that evening. Gillian seemed more troubled about the missing John Payne than she had any business being, but she was an intelligent woman and she knew about snakes. I don't think she believed my story completely.

Still, after a while, Gillian put away her computer and listened to Maggie's stories of Robert and the MC guys—the Swamp Hounds.

I couldn't imagine what Maggie's prim and proper mother would make of her only daughter deciding 'the one' was a motorcycle guy. But that was her problem to sort out.

I went to bed feeling a little better, or at least telling myself I did. Love made you foolish. I didn't need any of that. Juan would either come back or be gone forever. I didn't need him either.

Three weeks later, though, the ache in my chest each time I woke hadn't eased, and my skin was tighter. Sometimes, I found it hard to breathe. I was irritable and impatient with my roommates, and concentrating on my studies took all the energy I had to spare. I went to bed early every night, exhausted, and I cried into my pillow.

Maggie chose to do something about that. I wish she hadn't, but she meant well.

Chapter 18

I probably should have seen this coming.

ONE NIGHT, I came home from class to find Maggie and Robert sitting on the sofa. A rugged and handsome, tall blond with a red beard sat across from them in an arm chair, wearing tight jeans, a white V-neck t-shirt and a cut vest for the Swamp Hounds.

"Jenny! I'm so glad you're home." Maggie bounced up from where she'd been resting between Robert's legs as they reclined together on the sofa. I kept pretty regular hours, since I was doing nothing but forcing myself to study, so her extreme surprise I would be home just around six was poorly feigned. She'd counted on my being there on time. "I want you to meet James Matheson. He's President of the Swamp Hounds, and Robert's best friend."

To his credit, James was polite. He rose out of his chair to shake my hand in greeting, which seemed a little formal, but his grip was confident and he gave me a bright, warm smile that reached right up to his striking cyan blue irises. "Nice to meet you, Miss Banks," he said, with a deep southern drawl which told me he wasn't originally from Florida. Tennessee maybe? Alabama? I wasn't sure. I didn't have a good ear for it.

"Nice to meet you too," I said, trying to be polite before I let everyone down. "Enjoy your evening. I'm going to be in my room going over my notes. I've got an exam tomorrow."

"You can't go, Jenny!" Maggie insisted. "We've ordered loads of pizza and we have beer. Help us with that."

"I'm not really feeling very sociable, Maggie," I said. "My apologies to all of you."

"Nonsense!" Maggie pushed. "You have to have dinner anyway, right? Might as well share ours. You'll have to forgive Jenny," she said to James. "She's been a bit out of sorts for a while, which is why she needs to take a break and let her hair down. Right, Robert?"

"Can't hurt," Robert said, obviously not wanting to let his girl down while also trying not to push too hard. I couldn't help wondering why James was here. After all, he was genuinely a very good-looking guy. Didn't Motorcycle Clubs have many women hanging around waiting to join the men? At least, that was what I'd been led to believe by the stories I'd read and what I'd seen on television. A man like James shouldn't need a matchmaker like Maggie to hustle me on his behalf.

I decided I might as well sit with them, though. After all, I'd never hear the end of it from Maggie—or Gillian, probably. I put my books away in my room and came back out, sitting on the armchair next to James' across from Robert and Maggie.

For a while, it was a little awkward. Maggie was too eager for us to get to know each other and she decided the best way to do that was to tell us about ourselves. I learned James was from Atlanta and he had a master's degree in civil engineering from Georgia Tech. He'd checked all the broken roads of our great United States in person on his bike, before settling into a career. At some point, he'd met up with the former President of the Swamp Hounds, found the club lifestyle suited him, and settled in Florida. The former President had died of a stroke the year prior, so James was pretty new in his role, but his brothers respected him as a smart and level-headed guy. So Maggie said, and Robert agreed. James seemed a bit embarrassed. He kept hugging his beer bottle, not really drinking from it, and staring at his boots. Maggie's description of me was curious. She told James that I was a very dedicated psychology student, and that I came from a well-off family in Pennsylvania, involved in the railways. I had to cut her off and explain that we had been involved in trains once, but it was all absorbed by Amtrak long before my grandfather was born. Maggie didn't think that detail was as important as my family's wealth, which embarrassed me a bit.

"Why psychology?" James asked, and I knew he was just trying to be polite and cut Maggie off nicely before she mentioned how rich my family was again. Did the MC club need money for one of their charities? Was that what this was all about? I honestly would have given a donation for them to leave me alone. Still, James was being nice, so I answered him.

"The function of the mind is fascinating and unexplored," I said. "We think we understand human motivations and behavior, but we really don't. We've only scratched the surface on that. For too long, people tried to heal the physically ill but punished the mentally ill, so we're really very far behind on that, I think."

"Why not become a neurologist?"

"Well, while there *is* a physical aspect to brain function,

I'm more interested in the programming that impacts behavior."

"Don't let Jenny fool you, though," Maggie said. "She's smart, but she's also lots of fun to be with."

Honestly, I wanted to slap her.

"I don't doubt it," James said, smiling. Maggie passed me a beer, as if that would help me loosen up, which only made me tense up. I hadn't drunk alcohol in so long, except with Juan. I really didn't want it, but I was nervous and sad, and just… Well, I drank. After I finished the first, I drank a second. The conversation got livelier after that, with Maggie sharing stories of our party days, none of which painted me in a very good light, but I was beyond caring. I was about to start on a third beer when there was a knock on the door.

"Pizza's here!" Maggie cheered.

"I'll get it," I said, rushing to the door with the beer in my hand.

James rose to help me carry the pies. He stood really close behind me when I opened the door to find Juan standing there, in full dress uniform, looking all formal and fierce.

The minute he took in the sight of me holding a bottle with the biker Viking behind me, Juan turned away to head back down the hall without a word. I dropped the beer bottle and chased him. "Juan wait!"

He didn't stop, but I sped up my pace. "Juan Ruiz, you stop right this minute!" I shouted as he reached the end of the hall to wait for the elevator.

"Stay away from me, Jenny Banks," he growled. "I'm dangerous right now."

I didn't really hear him. I just leapt up to wrap my arms over his shoulders and my legs around his torso, trusting him to hold me up, which he did. He might have been angry, but he was also very glad to see me, going by the hot bar pressed up against his olive green pants as I pressed my lips against his. He let me kiss him, but he didn't let me in.

"I can't believe you're real," I said, speaking against his lips. "I'm… I thought you were gone!" I started crying. "You didn't even tell me you were back. Why didn't you send a message? Something! Oh, I'm so relieved to see you."

"Is that so, little slut?" he asked, all intense. "I come back to take you home and I find you drinking with another man."

"That was just a friend of Maggie's," I said. "I only just met him, like fifteen minutes ago."

"Don't lie to me, Jenny. I'd never forgive you for that."

"I swear! Take me back and ask if you don't believe me."

"You drank, though," he said.

"This is the first time I've had a beer in weeks, Juan Ruiz. And I only caved to peer pressure because I've been so sad and lost without you. I got tired of being sad. Where have you been? What the fuck took so long?"

"You don't want or need to know."

"Okay," I said. "Just take me home, then. Please?"

"No, I came to do something else, and now I'm not sure."

"What did you come to do?"

"Never mind, Jenny Banks," Juan said. "I made a mistake."

"No, you didn't and you know that! Stop it. Don't be mean to me. I've been miserable and I've been very good. You need to be nice."

"What the hell is going on?" Maggie asked behind us. "James is in there, all confused. Who is *this* guy?"

"I'm her man, and I'm taking my wife home," Juan said.

"You're *married*?" Maggie asked, completely shocked.

I was as surprised to hear it as she was. Even more surprised when I answered, "Not yet."

"Is this *John Payne*?"

"Who the fuck is John Payne, Jenny?" Juan asked.

I rolled my eyes at him. "Yeah, this is John," I said to Maggie. "I think he's taking me to a preacher-man now. So, like, enjoy your pizza with James and Robert. I'll be back for my things another day."

"You're a nut!" Maggie said, though she was smiling, so I decided not to take that too personally.

"She is," Juan said, as the elevator door opened. "I'm going to crack her open now."

As soon as the elevator door closed on a completely befuddled Maggie, Juan pressed me up against the wall of the elevator, with me still clasped around him like a rhesus monkey. I would not let him go. He tore into my mouth, an angry kiss which hinted at what he had in mind for me. I was in trouble and I didn't give a shit. I wanted all kinds of trouble from my strict Master. I was more than ready for that. "When I say you can't drink with any other man, little one, I mean it," he said, when we came up for air. "You were very naughty."

"I know, but you also were MIA."

"So every time I take a little while getting home, I should worry that you're going to misbehave?"

"No, because you're never allowed to be gone so long again without explaining yourself."

"I will never explain myself, Jenny Banks. Not for doing my duty."

"Okay," I said. "I can live with that."

"You're getting a whipping. You know that, right?"

"Yes, but you're also going to make me come, right?"

"Maybe."

I gave him my cutest pout, and he bit my lip, but not too hard.

"Why did you tease Maggie like that?" I asked.

"Who's Maggie?"

"My roommate, you know, upstairs."

"I wasn't teasing. I am going to crack you open."

"Yes, and I'm really looking forward to that, but I meant the other part."

"What other part?"

"Juan Ruiz, you know what I mean."

"We'll talk about that later."

"No, we'll talk about that now."

Just then, the elevator opened again, so he was right. We had to talk about it later. Before we could, we bumped into Gillian on the way out of the building.

"I fucking knew it!" she said, walking right past us after that.

"Do you know her?" Juan asked.

"Yeah, that's my other roommate."

"Seriously? I know that girl. She's an intern at the zoo. Doesn't like me much, I think."

"That is correct."

"Okay." Juan chuckled.

He carried me all the way to a waiting black limousine, with the driver holding the door open for us. Then Juan put me down only long enough for me to step inside, and after he joined me in the back seat, he pulled me over his lap.

"What are you doing?" I asked, giggling.

"Giving you the spanking you deserve," he said, landing the first swat on my butt as the driver closed the door. That stopped my laughter cold. Soon I felt the full force of Juan's irritation on my rump and was humiliated that the driver could see it in the rear-view mirror and hear each loud swat and every one of my whimpers as they landed.

"Ow-ow! I'm sorry I drank, okay? Ow! But I wasn't drunk. And honest… Ow! Seriously, that hurts! I haven't drunk the whole time you've been gone. Ow-ow! Please, stop! Ow!"

Juan stopped smacking, his hand apparently hurting as much as my butt at this point. He kneaded my butt like he planned to bake it. Honestly, it was hot enough you could say he'd already done that. "Where are we going?" I asked, sniffling.

"Home, but we have a pit-stop at another house first."

"Which house?"

"The White House."

"Seriously?"

"Yep."

"I'm not dressed for it."

"We'll get you appropriate clothes in DC tomorrow, right after we get our wedding license."

"I don't even have my purse, Juan! No IDs—nothing! And I will not marry you just because you say so."

"No?"

"No."

Juan lifted me up and placed me seated on his lap, resting in his muscular arms. He brought his hand to my chin and turned me to face him.

"You're mine, Jenny Banks."

"Yes, but…"

"No buts."

"Hold on a minute. We don't do relationships, remember? We don't do love."

"Where I was, I had a lot of time on my hands to think. You know what I thought?"

"What?"

"If I get out of this shit storm alive, I'm going to marry Jenny Banks."

"Why?"

"Because I *do* love you, stupid girl."

"Why?"

"Because you are the sexiest, smartest, sweetest little slut I've ever met. I look forward to spending time with you, no matter what we're doing. You're the only person on Earth I worry about. And the thought of any other man having you —*ever*—makes me want to kill."

"I'll make your life hell, you know."

"Probably. It's where I belong. Now, tell me the truth. Did you really miss me?"

"Yes, silly. I missed you awful. I thought you were dead!"

"I almost was."

"Well, that sucks."

"Yes, it sucks very much. But I survived, which sucks less. Now, marry me, Jenny Banks, or you'll have to explain to the President of the United States why you won't."

"Seriously? We're going to see the President?"

"Yes."

"Why?"

"He's going to give me something for my trouble."

"What?"

"A Medal of Honor."

"Really?"

"Yes, and you'll be there for the ceremony as my very well-behaved wife."

"I can't get a marriage license with no ID, Juan."

"We've got a plane waiting for us, you know."

"It will only take a minute."

"That asshole is probably still there. I don't want you getting distracted."

"James? He seems nice enough. That was just Maggie's doing, anyway. Nothing was going to happen, even if you were probably dead. I planned to wait until I knew for sure."

"What if you never knew?"

"Then I'd be waiting a long time."

"Sounds like something to me."

"Love? That's what Maggie said too. I didn't think so, but maybe she's right. The only man I've ever loved is my father, Juan. Some days I think that's not really love but pity. My father thought he loved my mother. Part of him probably still does, but she's incapable of love. I think I'm more like her than I'd like to be."

"You're not."

"No?"

"No."

"How would you know? You've never met her."

"I don't have to meet her to know who you are. I've met *you*. You're impetuous and you enjoy pain, so you put yourself through a lot, but you're also reliable and hardworking, and you have enough self-respect to prove people wrong about you. You're persistent, and creative, and headstrong. These are excellent qualities. But you're also tender, which makes you vulnerable. You've grown a shell to protect you. But that's not the same as being a cold and calculating killer, sweetness. Which is why you need me."

"I *do* need you," I said. "I'll admit that. I *also* need my IDs."

"Does that mean you agree to be my wife?"

"Yes."

"It won't be easy."

"I know, dummy. You're an *asshole*. That's what I love about you."

"I'm not sure why I'm flattered, Jenny Banks, but I'll take it," he said, kissing me softly.

Then Juan asked our driver to turn around so I could get my stuff and he went up to my dorm and stood in the way as James and Robert and Maggie and Gillian watched me grab my purse and a couple of other things I might want, and head out.

"She's not coming back," Juan told them, as I left the dorm.

"Juan, I didn't take *all* my stuff," I said, as we got to the elevator.

"I'll get the rest of your stuff. I don't want you going back to the dorms. Those girls are a bad influence on you."

"Come on, they're nice girls. They're my friends, you know."

"Not really," Juan said. "Only acquaintances. You couldn't trust them with your life."

"No, I guess not. Still…"

"You'll get your things. You'll finish your degree. Everything will be as it should be, but you'll be living with me from now on and following my orders. That's final."

"Yes, sir."

When the elevator opened for us again, he pressed me against the wall, his hand on my throat. "Now, say it."

"I love you."

"I love you more, Jenny Banks." Then he dove into my mouth with a dominant kiss that demanded my full submission.

That was it. I was ruined.

Epilogue

THREE YEARS *Later*

First, I thought I had the flu. It was going around. While I didn't have the sniffles, I was still tired every morning, and so the vomiting made sense. I couldn't keep any food down, or drink. It made Thanksgiving even more awkward. Mother was drunk. Dad was much better. Burt was great and so were his parents, who had finally moved into the house because his father wasn't up to taking care of their old house anymore. Burt's mother was really a very sweet woman, who kept insisting on trying to help the caterers with our Thanksgiving dinner, even though I told her they had it all under control. Juan was, as usual, a silent observer of the chaos of my family, but he wasn't judging, only watching me closely, offering me his support when I needed it most. That was mainly while I was hugging the toilet. He always held my hair out of the way.

"You need to see a doctor, Jenny Ruiz," he said. "Something is wrong."

"It's just a bug. It will pass."

"You listen to me," he said. "Tomorrow, if you're still throwing up, we're going to the hospital."

"Don't be so dramatic."

"Jenny, I know your body. Something is wrong."

"Okay, okay." I got up from the floor, still feeling woozy. "Jesus, you're bossy."

"That's because I'm the boss."

I stuck my tongue out at him and got a smack on the ass. Not too hard, though. Juan was really concerned.

"Dad likes you a lot, you know," I said, smiling at him. "He would like you less if he knew you spank me."

"He'd have to live with it. You need a spanking now and then, Jenny. More than most."

"Could you make me come instead? I'd really rather come than be spanked tonight."

"You don't behave that way."

"What? I was really a very good girl today. I drank nothing, no matter how often Mother filled my wine glass and then emptied it herself."

"Your mother is something else," Juan observed, with a grin.

"Yeah," I admitted.

"You are nothing like her. You aren't much like your dad, either. Though he's a decent and honorable man so I guess you inherited that, but you're stronger than either of them."

"Thanks, I guess."

"It was definitely a compliment, little one. Now, brush your teeth and let's get you to bed."

"For fun times?"

"Yes, baby," he said, kissing the top of my head and patting my butt.

We still had plenty of rough sex, which I absolutely loved, but never in my parents' house. Juan was also concerned that I was sick, so he made love to me gently, encouraging me to ride him a while before taking over. I came like a volcano. After we were done, I begged Juan to do it again, and he happily complied. Twice.

We stayed in one of the larger guest rooms whenever we visited my parents. We both fit more comfortably in the king-sized canopy bed than in the double-bed of my old bedroom. Besides, this room was far enough away from everyone else that it wouldn't matter if I made a little noise. Later that night, I heard a rustling and knocking on the windows, which looked out on the back patio. I got a weird feeling that it was Peter snooping on us. It creeped me out, but then Juan snuggled me close, like his teddy bear, and I fell back into a deep, blissful, dreamless sleep.

The next morning, Juan took me to the emergency room, ignoring my protests. He demanded that a doctor check me out. He was concerned that I was losing too many electrolytes and that I might collapse on him at any minute. Like I said, Juan can be melodramatic, especially when it comes to my well-being. It was nothing. Not even the flu. Just an ordinary, run-of-the-mill pregnancy.

"But she's on the pill," Juan told the young doctor who had run the test first thing.

"Well, something threw it off, maybe some other medication, or she missed a pill or two," the doctor said with a shrug. "It can happen."

As soon as he left us alone, I started crying.

"What's the matter, baby?" Juan asked.

"You're angry. You're disappointed in me."

"I am most definitely *not* angry *or* disappointed in you, Jenny Ruiz. You'd know if I was. I'm happy as a rooster at dawn, ready to crow about it to everyone and anyone who will listen. I'm going to be a father. That's just fucking awesome."

"I'm going to be a terrible mother."

"No, you're not. You'll be a wonderful mother. How many kids can say their mother is a licensed child psychologist?"

"Yeah, but they say psychologists make the worst parents because they're always analyzing their kids."

"Who says that?"

"I don't know."

Juan laughed. "You'll be fine, Jenny. It's both of us working through it, like everything else we do. A team. Got it?"

"Yes, sir."

"Good girl."

"Does this mean we don't get to play hard anymore?"

"Well, not while you're pregnant. We'll have to tone it down a bit. But I'll keep you satisfied, precious. Don't you worry about that."

Mother was extremely distressed to learn that she was going to be a grandmother. Dad was over the moon, slapping Juan's back and making big plans for Junior. I think it actually helped him a lot to have that to look forward to, but more credit goes to Burt for keeping Dad steady on his meds. He never went back into an asylum again. Mother was Mother. She always would be.

My water broke while Juan was putting the last of the shutters up on the old house in South Dade, which a new house twice over, rebuilt to perfection. I made a mess in the kitchen where I was busy boiling water and cursed a blue streak. "Fuck! Fuckity, fuckity fuck!"

Hurricane Wilson was only supposed to be a category two, but it had intensified on approach and we were bracing ourselves for the worst. I still had two weeks left to go, we thought, though I was big as a house. Junior obviously wanted out early. We still didn't know for sure whether we were having a boy or a girl because Juan wanted it to be a surprise, but the notion of Junior had stuck.

"Juan! Juan!" I called out, waddling over to the front of the house to get his attention. "It's time!"

Juan stopped what he was doing, leaving the window on one of the smaller bedrooms unprotected, and ran over.

"Now?"

"Yes."

"Fuck!" he agreed with me, which was nice but not very helpful. "We might not make it to the hospital, Jenny."

The winds were really picking up, and I had to agree with him on that. It was getting pretty dangerous to be on the road.

"Well, we don't have a choice, do we?"

"Fuck!"

"Okay, let's calm down," I said. "We have everything in the truck already on account of your thinking we should keep my bag in there just in case. You can drive through anything. We should just head out."

"I guess you're right."

We were halfway to the garage when the power went out.

"Fuck!" we said in unison.

"Changes nothing," Juan said. "We still have to go."

I agreed, except, just then, we heard a crack and a tremendous thump as the oak on our front yard tipped over, blocking our exit.

"Jesus fucking Christ," Juan said. "I guess you'll have the baby here."

"How?"

"Well, I'll have to help you deliver the baby."

"Can you do that?"

"I'm trained for just about everything but that. However, I have little choice. I'll get it done."

"Where?" But even as I asked, I knew the answer. The

only safe place would be the office behind the kitchen, where Juan had first found me. "I guess it's some kind of irony," I said, heading over to the secure but tiny room.

"Not really what the word means, Jenny," Juan said, flexing his literary muscle. "But it's definitely kismet."

As it was, Junior took fourteen hours to come out. We were all exhausted and sick of the back office, and Wilson was gone, by the time she uttered her first little wail against the fresh new world she'd popped into.

But the house held up. And it's holding still.

Amaryllis Lanza

Amaryllis Lanza took the road less traveled early on and has enjoyed many adventures in far flung places. She's settled for a while in the green and rolling countryside of Northern Europe where she shares her life with her lovely husband and her frolicking cats. When she's not writing (and reading) racy romance, suspense, and urban fantasy she works as a freelance writer. Her hobbies involve copious amounts of chocolate.

Visit her website here:
amaryllislanza.com

Don't miss these exciting titles by Amaryllis Lanza and Blushing Books!

Wild Horses of Lagrimas series
Her Bratva Cowboy

Billionaire Spy Series
Secrets and Seduction
Codes and Consequences
Pride and Punishment
The Unkindness
The Cauldron
The Watch
A Bounty of Blood and Betrayal

Jerks of Miami
Bound to the Jerk
Sinning with the Jerk
Temping with the Jerk
Hounded by the Jerk
Faking with the Jerk
Sheltered with the Jerk

Anthologies
12 Naughty Days of Christmas 2021